BONDS UNBROKEN

Mark E Gilligan, Ph.D.

Amelia,

I have loved teaching you this year. You have such a wonderful personality and great sense of humor. You also work extremely hard. I have no doubt that you will accomplish great things.

God Bless
Mark Gilligan
(Dr. G.)

The characters and events portrayed in this book are fictitious. Any similarity to real persons, living or dead, is coincidental and not intended by the author.

ISBN-13: 9798747192317
ISBN-10: 1477123456

Cover design by: Art Painter
Library of Congress Control Number: 2018675309
Printed in the United States of America

I dedicate this novella with love to my wonderful wife, Pam. My great children, Jaime, Patrick, Lauren, Molly, Alex, Brendan, and Abby. My grandson, Jesse Joseph and please God more to come. I am so grateful that you are in my life. You are everything to me.

And my fifth grade fantasticos: Daniel, Emery, Tess, Liam, Ross, Avery, Sloane, Amelia, Eden, Audrey, Edwin, Chloe, Liam, Blair, Nathan, and Audrey. You have made teaching this year such a joy. My love and prayers will go with you.

INTRODUCTION

"Bonds Unbroken" is an action packed, coming of age novella written in the style of Judy Blume and John Hughes. The book, which is set in 16th century Spain, follows the life of two friends, Diego Ramirez and Ferdinand Flores as they struggle with the complexities of faith, love, loss, family, and friendship during their transition from their carefree adolescence into adulthood.

A series of events entice the two friends to embark on a mission that they perceive to be simple and safe, only to find themselves entangled in a fight for human dignity and freedom. The struggle will test the boys' ciourage, faith, and sense of justice. This is a heartwarming story that will ask the readers to question important issues regarding justice and what it means to follow Jesus Christ truly.

"Knowledge which is divorced from justice may be called cunning rather than wisdom."

MARCUS TULLIUS CICERO

CONTENTS

CHAPTER ONE

"Summertime is always the best of what might be."

Charles Bowden

In the early morning, two fifteen-year-old boys sat together talking while sitting on a wall in Zaragoza, Spain. The year was 1526, and Europe was on the verge of the renaissance. The average life expectancy had risen to between thirty and forty years of age, and children were considered young adults at the tender age of sixteen. The world's population had exceeded four hundred million for the first time and included an estimated fifteen million inhabitants of the land that mapmakers had recently labeled the Americas. Michelangelo was creating magnificent works of art in Italy. Martin Luther had posted his thesis on the Cathedral in Germany, and the influential Catholic Church began to splinter off into several different denominations. That is except in Spain. France, Italy, and a few other countries where Catholicism reigned supreme. Profound changes were taking place all over the known world, but as typical for teenagers their age, the boys' focus was only on their upcoming summer break, which was scheduled to begin at the end of classes that day.

"I know one thing for certain," remarked Diego as he and

his friend Ferdinand picked up their books and began their walk to school. "Juan Vasquez will be starting his summer holidays missing a few teeth and perhaps sporting a bloody nose."

"Great," responded Ferdinand, " and you will begin your break with a whipping from your father and a grounding from your mother that will leave nobody to celebrate the beginning of summer with me. No way. I don't need or want you to fight on my account. Just leave it alone."

"Leave it alone!" roared Diego. "Leave it alone! You must be daft! Do you think for one moment after what he did to you yesterday that I would not beat him up today? I should have done it much sooner, but yesterday he went too far. No one humiliates my best friend and gets away with it, especially in front of girls. We both know that the headmaster would have flogged him good yesterday if the big coward had not lied about what he had done. But believe me, a spanking from the headmaster is nothing compared to what he has coming from me."

"That is not how I want to handle this at all," said Ferdinand. "Furthermore, I don't want you to sin by striking someone on my account. Life has a way of balancing things out. Let's just leave it in God's hands."

"God's hands? God's hands?" Diego exclaimed with frustration. "Maybe God put Juan in the headmaster's hands for what he did, and you just went and let him go. With the whole class so outraged that they were all ready to back your story -- or what should have been your story--which is something they usually were too afraid to do because the brute is such a bully, Mr. P was ready to get out the switch. If only you had corroborated the truth, but instead, you said nothing. What was Mr. Pellizzaro to do when the victim refused to talk, except to let the big brute off with a warning? I will never figure you out, Ferdinand. Why wouldn't you let Mr. P give Juan what he deserved, and then you wouldn't have to worry about me knocking the devil out of him?"

"I had to let him go, Diego, because I forgave him."

"Forgave him?" asked Diego incredulously. "When did he

apologize?"

"He didn't apologize. Like the soldiers who completely stripped Jesus of all of his clothes and did a lot worse, did not apologize, but he still forgave them. So I forgave Juan. It wasn't easy, but I did it, and I can't have you going on and beating him up, or my act of forgiveness will not count. So please, Diego," Ferdinand begged. "Promise me that you won't lay a finger on Juan when we get to school."

"You can be the most frustrating person in the whole world. Do you know that?" But Diego promised as he put his large arm over his little friend's shoulders, "I will not lay a finger on him." As he did so, he took a certain measure of solace because while promising not to lay a finger on Juan, he never promised not to figure out some other way to avenge his buddy. As the two walked, a delightfully sinister plan began to worm its way into Deigo's head. He contrived a scheme that would bring retribution to Juan for his vulgar and embarrassing action against Ferdinand. If it worked, it would humiliate Juan and bring down on him the headmaster's rightful wrath. As the two friends rounded the last turn heading for Our Lady of the Pillar School, Ferdinand smiled to himself. "Good," he thought. "Twenty minutes before they opened the doors." He would have time to put his plan into motion. "Mary, Our Lady of the Pillar, I need your help on this one," Diego prayed to himself and made the sign of the cross in his mind.

CHAPTER TWO

"When life hands you dirt, plant seeds."

MATSHONA DIHLWAYO

As they neared the schoolyard, Isabelle Lopez and Rosalie Finara, two of the boys' classmates and dear friends since their early years of school, approached them. Although neither of them would ever admit it, except to each other, the two boys had for several years hoped that their friendship with the girls would evolve into something more. In their private conversations Diego and Ferdinand agreed that the old axiom, "Opposites attract." certainly did apply in their case. Diego, the outgoing and athletic boy, was drawn to the quiet, reserved, and studious Rosalie. Ferdinand, dedicated, respectful, and very scholarly, was attracted to the gregarious and often impulsive Isabelle. "If for some reason, I cannot become a priest and serve my God," he often confided to Diego, "Then Isabelle is exactly the kind of girl that I could marry."

Even as they acknowledged that they were attracted to girls who were so vastly different from them, the boys never really thought how different they were from each other. They had simply been best friends since before they could even walk. Perhaps the fact that they were neighbors and their parents were friends played a huge role in their friendship, but somehow the boys always felt that, like two opposite sides of a magnet, providence would have drawn them to each other anyway.

"Hi guys," Isabelle said as the two girls neared. "Even that stupid idiot is smart enough not to show up early this morning. I imagine that he won't show until the bell rings and everyone goes inside. He knows what's going to happen when you get your hands on him, Diego. Why, if he were here, I probably would not have even waited for you. I would have darkened his eye myself."

"Diego has already promised me that he won't lay a hand on Juan," declared Ferdinand. "I certainly don't want either of you to touch him on my behalf either. I have chosen to turn the other cheek."

"Literally?" asked Isabelle amusingly. "It seems like we saw you turn both cheeks yesterday after Juan pulled your pants down in front of the whole class."

"Not funny." groused Ferdinand. "Not funny at all."

"Ferdinand is right," Diego said; I have promised not to lay a hand on Juan, and I don't think you should either."

"Thank you," Ferdinand replied as he headed off to see what type of seeds Gorges, the handyman, was planting in the back garden. "I'll meet you all inside."

As soon as Ferdinand turned his back, both girls turned their gazes on Diego. "Diego? You plan on letting Juan get away with the embarrassing antics he pulled on Ferdinand yesterday!" Isabelle exclaimed, barely keeping her emotions in check. "You know that fear of you is the only thing that prevents Juan from making Ferdinand's life miserable. He teases him mercilessly when you are not around. Once he realizes that he can get away with a disgusting stunt like that without you doing anything, then Ferdinand's life will be unbearable." She could not hide her obvious concern for her friend, and Diego got the first hint that perhaps Ferdinand's feelings for her might be mutual.

"I didn't say that I wasn't going to do anything to him," Diego smiled impishly. "I only said that I would not lay a hand on him."

The three friends huddled together as Diego explained his plan to the girls and talked about their role. Soon Isabelle and Rosalie were sharing Diego's excitement for the scheme as they eagerly agreed to do their part. "That is the craziest, most brilliant idea that I ever heard," exclaimed Isabelle.

"We're in!" added Rosalie with a determined look on her face.

Then they split up to set the plan in motion. The girls started toward the front of the school to distract Mr. Pelizzaro, the headmaster, while Diego crept to the building's side, taking cover behind the overgrown shrubs that grew there.

CHAPTER THREE

"Planning is bringing the future into the present so that you can do something about it."

ALAN LAKEIN

As the two girls approached Mr. Pelizzaro, nothing seemed amiss. Mr. P. was well-liked by his students, and he genuinely cared about them. Even though occasionally he had to resort to whippings when students stepped out of line, it was evident to everyone that witnessed the spectacles that it truly pained him much -- perhaps even more than the student on the receiving end of the paddle. He was strict when he had to be and had a fun side, which made his students respect him and feel comfortable around him. So when Rosalie and Isabelle walked up to him and asked him for suggestions for what they and their families should do on a planned summer holiday to Italy, he was more than happy to oblige.

It was well known to the school's families that their headmaster loved Italy and especially Florence, the center of the Renaissance and home to the famous Medici Family. The revival was not only a rebirth of the classical arts. It was also the rebirth of classical education in Western Europe. After Mr. Pelizarro had shut down the school for the year, he would travel to Florence for a two-week stay each summer. Upon returning, he always brought great ideas to his teachers on teaching Latin, rhetoric, science, or mathematics. He also bought small pieces of his favorite art form, which like most art, was produced in Florence; He loved little pewter figurines. He was intrigued by the pieces' strength and the incredible detail that the artists etched into each piece. Of course, an added benefit was that the pewter pieces were more affordable than most other art forms, which was a significant consideration to a man who had to survive on an educator's income.

Over the years, his collection, which he proudly displayed outside of his office, slowly grew. School families who traveled to Florence would occasionally bring him back pieces as a token of appreciation for his exemplary work educating their children. His collection became considerable in time, and people would often bring visiting relatives to see it. Even the mayor was impressed by the display and would bring important dignitaries. Mr. P was always gracious and pleased to share his collection with whoever wanted to see it.

The two friends listened to their headmaster's suggestions as intently as they were able, considering the mixture of guilt and excitement that was whirling inside their heads. When they saw Diego emerge from the side of the school, they thanked Mr. P for his advice, politely excused themselves, and nonchalantly headed off to meet their friend. "I am more than happy to get even with Juan, but I feel bad for having misled Mr. P. I do like him," said Isabelle.

"Me too," agreed Rosalie. And both girls decided that if either of them ever did make it to Florence, they would have to bring him back a piece of pewter.

"Are we set?" asked Rosalie when the three were united again.

"I hope so," replied Diego. "There is a lot that could go wrong, but hopefully, Our Lady of the Pillar will intercede for us." The three friends then bowed their heads and said a quick Hail Mary.

Just then, the bell rang, and the three-headed toward the

building. It was now time for the two girls to implement stage two of the plan.

CHAPTER FOUR

"Creativity is intelligence having fun."

ALBERT EINSTEIN

The small classroom was chaotic as it usually was that time every morning. The students were allowed fifteen minutes to put their things away and sort themselves before the teacher would enter the room, bringing the quiet and structure necessary to start the day's instruction.

The actual process, especially for the older students, took about five minutes, so they used the remaining time to visit with friends. Isabelle wasted no time letting Juan know just how she felt about his latest attack on Ferdinand. As soon as he turned around after depositing his things in his cubby, she let him have it. "Of all the stupid and ignorant things that I have seen you do throughout the years, that was by far the most disgusting. Why would you do something like that? Did you think it would be funny? It wasn't. It was horrible." She continued, not allowing Juan an opportunity to speak.

Juan looked around and felt even before he saw all eyes focused on him. "The heck with him if he is not able to take a joke. Where is the runt, anyway?" asked Juan, not seeing Ferdinand in the class.

"It wasn't a joke; it was just plain cruel," Isabelle shouted back, unable to keep her emotion in check, which played well into the planned scene. " And as the student with the highest marks for the year, Ferdinand is in the headmaster's office preparing the summer farewell address. Something he has had the honor of doing the past three years and something you would never have to worry about doing. And for the record, Ferdinand is at least three times the man that you are. Is that why you are always picking on him? Is it because you are jealous that he can do just about anything better than you?"

That statement bothered Juan as he was attracted to Isabelle. He suspected that she had feelings towards Ferdinand, which was the very reason he had tormented him for so long. Unfortunately, the more he abused him and the better Ferdinand endured gracefully, the more Isabelle was drawn to Ferdinand, and the more she despised Juan. "What do you mean? There is nothing he can do better than me? You are talking crazy, and you know it!"

"Oh, sure, you can be more mean, but what else?" Isabelle continued. "He is much smarter, more handsome, and can even run faster and jump higher than you."

"You have to be kidding me," Juan snorted. "Other than possibly Diego on his best day, everyone knows I am the fastest boy in the class, and what makes you think that short elf can jump?' Why he couldn't even jump over an anthill."

It was Rosalie's turn to enter the fray. "Because we saw him. Didn't we, Isabelle? As we were walking out of school yesterday, Ferdinand was on about how he had been practicing his jumping and could touch Mary's toes," she explained, talking about the statue of Our Lady of the Pillar that hung in the hall. "He said it was his way of saying good-bye to her every day after school. We thought that he was just putting us on, but he did it. Oh, it took three tries, and he barely touched it, but he did. It was quite amazing."

Juan boastfully declared, "If Ferdinand could barely touch the statue after three tries, then I can easily palm the statue on my very first attempt." Juan was bolstered by the fact that he was at least eight inches taller than Ferdinand, maybe more.

"Okay, let's see you try," came dares from all of the class who were now engaged in the exchange.

"I am sure that Mary would not allow a shameless heathen like you even to touch a statue of her." snapped Isabelle.

"It will be perfect timing," said Rosalie. "Right after the final assembly today, Mr. P will go out front like he always does to say goodbye to everyone. We will just hang back for a few minutes. It won't take long, right, Juan? Remember you said you could do it on your first try."

Juan thought about it a minute. "Nah," he said, " I know I can do it, no sweat, but it's a stupid thing to do, and after the accusations yesterday getting to Mr. P, I think I should lay low for a little while. "

"Just as well," said Isabelle, "We all could get in trouble if for some reason Pelizzaro did catch Juan. There isn't any way that he has the fortitude that Ferdinand has not to snitch on us all."

This remark sent Juan off. "There is no way that I need to snitch on anyone," he screamed. You are right. Even if Ferdinand is a little runt, he was man enough not to go running to Pelizzaro. There is no chance that I ever would. You can count on that. I just don't want to take a chance right before the break. Now leave me alone."

The other kids chided him and urged him to give it a go if he was sure that it would be so easy, but he was not budging. It seemed like the whole plan was for naught when Rosalie spoke up. "What if we make things interesting?'

The class grew silent. "Go ahead, I'm listening," responded Juan, intrigued.

"Well," said Rosalie. "Tomorrow night Diego is taking me to the concert in town. Diego was astonished to hear this proclamation but could hardly contain his excitement. "If you can touch even the base of the statue the first time, then you can take Isabelle to the concert." (Isabelle was quite the opposite of excited to hear this pronouncement.) If, however, you fail, or should I say when you fail, because Mary will not let you succeed, you have to promise before all of us that you will forever leave Ferdinand alone and tell Mr. Pelizzaro the truth about what you did yesterday."

"And most importantly, I do not have to go out with you," added Isabelle with a disgusted look on her face.

The thought of actually going out in public with Isabelle was just too much for Juan to turn down. "Besides, what could go wrong?" He thought. "Did they think that Mary would intercede to prevent him from touching the statue? Surely the Mother of God had more important things to worry about?"

The whole event should take no more than a few seconds, and with Mr. P distracted saying his good-byes, he would never know. If Ferdinand were able to touch that thing, he would easily be able to reach it.

After the class agreed that no one would alert Mr. P to what was going on or interfere in any way other than to pray to Mary, he readily agreed.

CHAPTER FIVE

"The idea of waiting for something makes it more exciting."

ANDY WARHOL

The last day of term's excitement always made that day seem longer than two days put together. This final day, however felt like a whole week of days all rolled into one for the three friends. At last, the lunch bell rang, and the class was dismissed to the garden area to eat their lunch.

As Ferdinand meticulously put his books and pencils away, as he always did, Diego, Rosalie, and Isabelle preceded him outside. "That was brilliant acting, said Diego to the girls. And the idea of the bet to push him over the top was brilliant, Rosalie."

"Ha, brilliant?" sneered Isabelle giving her friend a menacing stare, "You both better pray hard that this works. Because if it does not, and I have to go on a date with that, that, whatever the worst thing in the world is, I will spend the rest of my life making sure your lives are miserable." Diego and Rosalie exchanged sideways glances, and each crossed themselves and then crossed their fingers.

As each of their classmates walked past them, they crossed themselves or murmured that they were praying too, all except Juan. When Ferdinand finally joined them, all references to the bet ceased. Before finalizing negotiations on the terms of the bet, the girls made Juan and the entire class promise that Ferdinand would not know about the wager in advance. Isabelle had said that, as pious as her friend Ferdinand was, it would give them too much of an advantage If he were to add his prayers to theirs. In reality, all three friends were concerned about Ferdinand figuring out that they had contrived some plan to punish Juan, and besides, they were sure that he would not approve of any project that involved using the Holy Mother.

Instead, the group began laying out their summer plans, and shortly after finishing the food, the bell rang to go back in. "Great," murmured Rosalie, "The only part of the day to move too fast is lunch."

As the four of them cleaned up their area in preparation for heading in, Juan joined them. He didn't say anything; he simply stopped in front of Isabelle, winked, and mouthed a kiss. In turn, Isabelle turned to Rosalie and glared.

"What is that about?" asked Ferdinand. Even as he asked the question, the realization came to him that he could tolerate much from Juan in the name of Jesus Christ, but Ferdinand wasn't sure how much he could handle if Juan ever started picking on Isabelle.

"Nothing, just Juan being obnoxious as always," said Diego placing his arm over his friend's shoulder in his customary fashion. "Let's just leave it in the hands of Mary, Our Lady of the Pillar." And the four returned to the class

The afternoon did move more quickly than the morning because all the students did mainly was recover books. Although it had almost been one hundred years since the printing press's invention, books were costly and hard to get. The teacher took care to ensure that the books would still be suitable for the next class.

After wrapping the books in new covers, the students devoted the rest of the time to cleaning desks, slates, erasers, and floors. Before they knew it, the teachers were herding the class to the grassy area behind the school building for Ferdinand's final address and the closing prayer.

Ferdinand always kept the final address short for three reasons. First, he was a gifted orator; he knew that the most compelling talks were concise. Secondly, this was the third time in a row that he gave the address as the school's top student and didn't know what he could say that the older students hadn't already heard, And most importantly, he knew his audience. Every student would be grateful for brevity as they excitedly awaited the final dismissal of the year. So he spoke briefly about gratitude to Mr. Pellizzaro and the teachers. The blessing of the friendships that had been formed and nurtured throughout the year. The need to study and stay sharp over the summer -- only he would do that. He cautioned his schoolmates to keep safe and ended by singing the praises of the school's namesake, Mary, the Lady of the Pillar who, while living in Jerusalem, appeared to the Apostle James in that very town. He implored her intercession upon the entire community as they parted for the summer.

Fr. Alberta, the parish priest, then gave his official blessing. Fr. Alberta, or Fr. Albatross as the kids not so affectionately called him because he resembled one, was not nearly as good of a speaker as Ferdinand. For someone not gifted with the ability to speak, the priest certainly loved to hear the sound of his own voice. As he said his first words, the students all hung their heads and closed their eyes, mimicking piety as they patiently waited for his words to pass with their minds on any number of things other than the words spoken. Finally, at the appropriate time, those still awake responded, "Amen!" and all the students opened their eyes and lifted their heads in unison.

Mr. P then briefly wished the students a fond farewell and gave final instructions. They were to remain there until he and the teachers had a chance to take up their positions around the front. Then the older students would direct the rest of the students, beginning with the youngest, through the building and out the front doors. It was a noisy, joyous proceeding with much screaming and hollering as the students half walked and half-ran through the line of teachers to freedom.

Diego and the girls ignored Ferdinand's prompting to "get a move on it" while they and the rest of the class lagged behind the crowd of happy students. He did not realize that the class still had a final bit of business to attend before heading off.

CHAPTER SIX

"There are two ways to live your life. One is as though nothing is a miracle. The other is as though everything is a miracle."

ALBERT EINSTEIN

"What's going on?" Ferdinand asked as the class suddenly stopped short and formed a semi-circle around Our Lady of the Pillar statue, and everyone except him and Juan started to pray.

"One final prayer," whispered Diego. "Your talk got to us."

Ferdinand was even more surprised when Juan moved back from the group about six feet and started to stretch. "You are all pathetic!" Juan said, looking around at the class, and "Be ready after lunch tomorrow," he said explicitly to Isabelle. Then Juan started his approach. He swung his arms. His form and timing were perfect. He launched from his strong foot, and the angle was perfect. Then...

"BOOM!" a huge sound followed by a deafening silence.

"She e e e moved," stuttered a shocked girl named Maria,one of only five girls in the class.. "She moved!"

One by one, as the class emerged from their silent stupor, they began to cross themselves and started, "Hail Mary, full of grace ...."

Mr. Pelizzaro and the teachers came sprinting into the

school to see what had caused the incredible bang. The group gasped, stunned by what they saw. In front of them, an entire class of fifteen-year-olds struggled to recover from the effects of a significant shock. Immediately outside Mr. Pelizzaro's office, pewter figurines were strewn around the beautiful statue of Our Lady of the Pillar. Whatever had happened, neither the sculpture nor the figures were harmed by the incident as both were made from solid material. The same could not be said about the blubbering student on his knees in the middle of the chaos, who was no doubt transformed forever.

"I can't believe it! I can't believe it!" Juan Marcos stammered while he crossed himself. "I didn't even touch her! She moved out of the way! No, she dove away from my mere touch! Oh Mother Mary, Oh Mother Mary," he cried. "I am so sorry. I will be better, and I won't be mean anymore. Please forgive me." he pleaded.

Then Juan, pulling himself together just a little, noticed Mr. P. and the other teachers for the first time. "Mr. Pelizarro, I am sorry for the mess. It was all my fault. I will pick it all up and return the statue to her proper place. I will be a better person next year. You will see, but you will have to punish me good for what I did yesterday. I did pull down Ferdinand's pants in front of everyone, and then I lied about it," he confessed.

Then Juan turned and faced Ferdinand. "I have been horrible to you. Not just yesterday but for a long time. Is there any way that you can forgive me?"

"I already have," Ferdinand quietly replied as he turned and headed out the door into the afternoon light. Suddenly he stopped. turned, and headed back towards Juan.

Everyone wondered, "Is this it? Was Ferdinand, after so much abuse, finally going to let his tormentor have it?" But Ferdinand said nothing. He simply stooped down and started to help Jaun clean up the mess. Speechless, the rest of the class joined in the effort.

CHAPTER SEVEN

"Coincidence is God's way of being anonymous."

LAURA PENDERSEN

As soon as the four friends said their goodbyes to their classmates and conversed about the fantastic event they had witnessed, they set off down the road. When they had put some space between them and the others, Ferdinand stopped and turned to the others. "Okay, out with it," he demanded.

"Out with what?" said Diego feigning innocence. "You of all people, Ferdinand, should believe in miracles. What, you think miracles only happen to others?"

"Yes, I do believe in miracles. And having witnessed such a dramatic change in Juan Marcos, I do believe that a miracle of sorts may have occurred here today. But I want to know what sort of miracle may or may not have happened and what you three had to do with it. Explanations, please," said Ferdinand eyeing each one of them in turn.

"What makes you think that we had anything to do with it?" asked Diego.

"Three things," said Ferdinand in his matter-of-fact, logical way. "First, I might have been born at night, but it wasn't last night. I know you all, and the likelihood of Juan doing what he did to me yesterday and what happened to him today without you having some part to play in it is minuscule."

"Secondly, you have all been acting strangely today. Every time Juan made some type of insinuation that you and he were going out, Isabelle, it ate me up inside and made me want to vomit." This statement both surprised and pleased Isabelle.

"And finally," pronounced Ferdinand as if he were a lawyer laying out his case, "When I was checking out the plants behind the school, Diego, I saw you sneaking behind the bushes, and we both know the only reason why you would be rummaging around back there."

"Okay, okay," said Diego acquiescing to his friend's demand for an explanation. "We both know I was going to tell you sooner than later, anyway. I never could keep a secret from you for long, but please try not to be mad."

Ferdinand, Isabella, and Rosalie jumped up on a wall that bordered the road, careful to avoid a patch of nettles growing nearby, as Diego began to explain the events of the day.

While the girls distracted Mr. Pelizzaro, Diego stealthily lifted the side window and hoisted himself into the school building. As had been suggested by Ferdinand, this was not the first time he had used this window to either access the building or escape it, and he had become quite adept at it. During his days at the school, he did it so often that Ferdinand jokingly had started to refer to the window as "Diego's Door."

Once inside the window, Diego found himself in the familiar confines of the boys' restroom. He checked the stalls. Finding them empty, he quietly stepped to the door and slowly opened it. Looking both ways to make sure the coast was clear, Diego quietly ventured forth through the corridor that led to the headmaster's office. He stopped at the janitor's closet to grab a small ladder and a screwdriver on his way to his destination.

Diego stopped at the beautiful wooden statue of Our Lady of Pillar, which hung high above and slightly to the left of the beloved pewter collection. Mr. Pelizzaro used to joke that Mary was standing guard over his art collection.

Diego worked quickly and quietly. He climbed the ladder

and loosened the screws to the base on which the statue stood, not enough that she would fall --he hoped -- but enough that it would not take much for her to come plummeting down. When finished, Diego hurried down the steps and returned the tools on his way out the same window through which he entered.

After Diego had laid out his actions in preparation for the scheme, Isabelle and Rosalie took turns explaining how they baited Juan into the trap. When Rosalie came to the part about how she enticed Juan into taking the bet by offering up a date with Isabelle, she received a sharp elbow to the ribs from her friend. "I still haven't forgiven you for that, by the way. Boy, are you lucky it worked?"

"I am not sure that luck had all that much to do with anything," interjected Diego. "You see, I had to work fast this morning. I had no way of knowing how loose to make the screws. Not loose enough, and she might not fall when tapped by Juan. Too loose, and she might come tumbling down too soon. We knew that neither the statue nor the figurines would be in any real danger, because they were both made from such strong material. So while the others prayed that Mary would miraculously move to avoid Juan's hand, we were praying that she would remain up there until he touched it. It was beyond our wildest hopes that she would stay up there until Juan **almost** touched her and then come tumbling down. I don't know if it were from the vibrations created when he jumped or truly a miracle? But what are the chances? What do you think, Ferdinand?"

Ferdinand mused, "God often works miracles through everyday occurrences and things that people might consider coincidences. Today's events might just be one of those times, especially if Juan's transformation is genuine as it appeared to be."

"So," asked Isabelle looking into Ferdinand's eyes, "Are you angry with us?"

"Yes," Ferdinand responded. "I mean no, I mean no, oh, I don't know. I mean, I want to be. I think I should be, but I just feel really, really, happy to be blessed with such wonderful friends."

Isabelle smiled at him, and the four-headed off down the road. "So, Diego," asked Rosalie, when are you going to pick me up tomorrow?" Diego looked at her quizzically. "Well, you heard me tell everyone that you are taking me to the concert tomorrow. You wouldn't make a liar out of me, would you?"

Now it was Diego's turn to be speechless for once in his life. "And after what we did for you today," added Isabelle turning to Ferdinand, "You better believe that you are taking me to the concert also."

Stunned, the two boys looked at each other with amazement and smiles that spanned their faces. "Uh, we have something to confess to you," Diego began before Rosalie interrupted.

"We know, we know already," said Rosalie smiling at Isabelle. "You know, Isabelle, for a guy who just orchestrated such an ingenious plan and the guy who consistently has earned top marks at school, these two can be pretty slow picking up clues."

"We certainly do have our work cut out for us." agreed Isabelle as she put her hand in Ferdinand's. Diego took her cue and grabbed Rosalie's hand as the four of them headed down the road.

CHAPTER EIGHT

"It was the best of times, it was the worst of times...."

CHARLES DICKENS, "A TALE OF TWO CITIES"

Every teenaged person deserves to experience that one memorable summer that they will never forget. A summer that they will carry in their hearts forever. The beginning of that summer showed promise of being that summer for the four friends who had now also become two couples. School was out for what seemed like an eternity to the young. Often boys who reached sixteen considered their formal education finished, and girls usually didn't even go that long, but all four of their parents highly valued education. They knew that they were going to turn sixteen shortly and enter that which, at that time, would be considered adult age, but as the summer sun heated the earth and love was in the air, their focus was only on the present.

That initial date at the concert turned out to be a wonderful experience for all. Although it seemed like it would be awkward at first, the two couples seemed to transition from four great friends to four great friends who were also two couples, seamlessly and comfortably. Numerous schoolmates, seeing the pairs holding hands, commented, "It's about time you guys got together," or " I was wondering when you were going to see what we all saw for a long time," or "You belong together.". Even Mr. P and a few of the teachers made comments along the same lines.

Other than when they first started, the only awkward moment was when the four reached Rosalie's house on their way home and stopped a short distance from the door. It was evident that neither she nor Diego knew how to say goodbye, should there be a kiss involved? Ferdinand and Isabelle were no less anxious, knowing that they would find themselves in the same predicament shortly. Finally, after a few moments of silence, Rosalie let go of Diego's now sweaty hand, walked over to Ferdinand and Isabelle, and hugged each one. Then she grabbed Diego's hand again and motioned for him to walk her up to the door. Once there, after making plans to get together the next day, she kissed him once quickly and softly on the lips and went inside.

Diego returned to the two as if he were walking on air. The other couple seemed equally relieved to have a sample to follow when they reached Isabelle's house. After Ferdinand took his leave from Isabelle, the two boys walked back to their homes. Neither of them spoke. They didn't need words. Both knew each other so well they knew what each other was feeling. They knew it was the same as they were feeling, and they were happy and happy for each other.

CHAPTER NINE

"An ideal world inhabited by carefree people is nothing more than a utopia."

ERALDO BANOVAC

Part of the charm of a magical summer is not that there is something new to do every day, but that the same specialness continues day after day until you reach the point that you no longer even know one day from another. That is how the summer flowed, at least for the most part, for Diego and Ferdinand. Both boys would rise early with their parents and head off with their fathers to their stores on the banks of the Ebro. The beautiful river bisected the city, flowing from the northwest region through the southeast section.

Working with their fathers in the shops made each boy feel useful, productive, and grown-up. They loved interacting with the customers, most of whom they knew, and learning the businesses. Mostly, however, they loved spending time with their fathers. While neither of them liked the idea, they both knew that at some point, these unique, daily times with their fathers would become less frequent as they took on their own responsibilities.

The four workers would often set out together to the river, depending on what each had to accomplish before the start of business. On such occasions, the boys would always walk about ten feet behind their fathers, talking. When they reached Ramirez's Fine Leather shop on the east side of the river, the group would split, Diego and his father would go in and start preparations. Ferdinand and Mr. Flores would continue to their restaurant, which sat just over the bridge on the river's west side.

The two fathers had arranged it so that their sons would always have their lunch simultaneously, which they ate sitting on the bridge with their legs dangling over the edge. On rare occasions, Isabelle or Rosalie, or on even more rare occurrences, Isabelle and Rosalie would be able to break away from their chores at home and join them for lunch.

The neighbors would almost always walk home together in the late afternoon for dinner. Then Diego and Ferdinand would sneak off to pick up the girls. Sometimes they would stay at one of their houses talking and laughing until it was time to go home. Occasionally they would play silly games together, such as cards or Alquerque, an ancient Arabic game remnant of the Moor invasion.

Sometimes they simply walked hand in hand along the banks of the river. And on those sweltering Spanish nights, they occasionally jumped into the river at their favorite swimming spot, isolated from the city itself. Afterward, they would dry off while lying on the ground, stargazing and talking.

As reliable as the rising and setting of the sun, this pattern repeated itself every weekday. Saturday and Sundays were different, however. On Saturdays, the boys were excused from their duties at the store by noon, and the girls were set free from their chores soon after. Saturday afternoon was usually the time that the two couples had to spend time alone. They typically did the same things as a couple as they did when the four were together, but this time alone was essential and much coveted. During this time, the couples could have deep conversations and learn each other's regrets, fears, thoughts, and dreams. The pair would then join one of their families for dinner before setting out to join up with the other couple.

It was on just such an occasion that the first chink in the armor of the otherwise magical summer came to light. Diego and Rosalie had been swimming in the Ebro before going to Rosalie's house for dinner. Ferdinand and Isabelle had been talking turns nodding off in each other's arms before going back to Isabelle's house for dinner.

"What's wrong?" asked Ferdinand as Diego and Rosalie approached Isabelle and him at their designated meeting spot on the bridge. Both Ferdinand and Isabelle sensed more than knew something was wrong with their dear friends, even before they had fully arrived. When they got closer, the couple's feelings were confirmed. It was apparent that both of them had been crying hard.

Before explaining the situation, Rosalie ran and took comfort in the arms of her childhood friend. "Oh, Isabelle," she wept. "At dinner tonight, Mom and Dad announced that we were going to move back to Tudela. Dad has received a wonderful job offer there, and both sets of my grandparents are getting older. Mom and Dad want to be closer so that they can take care of them. They wanted to tell Diego and me together because they know how hard this is going to be for both of us, but they truly feel that it is the right thing to do."

"I want to hate them for what they are doing or be mad, but I know that it is the right thing for them to do," said Rosalie stepping out of Isabelle's embrace. "They are not selfish; they are selfless. They are right, though; this is so hard for us all. Sometimes it stinks growing up. If I was still a little kid, I could throw and tantrum and stubbornly refuse to go. I hate having to be mature."

Rosalie then looked Ferdinand in the eyes. "You know," she said, "I never had any brothers, but as we have grown so close throughout the years and especially this summer, you are my brother. "Except," she said, reconsidering, "You are dating Isabelle, who is truly a sister to me, and that would be yuck. I mean."

Ferdinand interrupted her laughing warmly and breaking

up the somber mood just a little, "I love you too, Rosalie." he replied.

She responded with a warm embrace.

"Well," said Isabelle, trying to pull herself together and trying to be positive, "Tudela is slightly less than a day's coach ride away. It's not like you are moving to America or anything."

"Yes," added Ferdinand, "and we will all write and visit when we can." And you can come and visit us. Our friendship is too strong to let a little bit of distance break it up."

"Plus," exclaimed Rosalie, beginning to wipe away her tears, "We don't leave until the last week in August, and Mom and Dad said that I could come back for Fiestas Del Pilar. Oh, I might not stay for the whole nine days, but I will be here on 12 October and several days before. I can't think of anything more fun than sharing the parades and fireworks with my best friends in the world," she said, looking at Ferdinand and Isabelle. "And of course," she added, " The man that I love," she said, looking deeply into Diego's sad-looking eyes. Diego struggled but succeeded in putting on a brave smile for the woman he loved.

"That is," added Rosalie, almost as an afterthought,' If I would be able to stay with you and your family, Isabelle."

Isabelle just laughed. "If you ever tried to stay somewhere else," she mused, "I think I would have to slap you in the face." Both girls laughed as Rosalie embraced Diego, who had remained very quiet, unsure of what to say and full of emotions.

Sensing that the two needed some more time together as a couple, Isabelle placed her arm around Ferdinand's waist, and the two of them headed arm in arm down the path that ran along the river. "We will see you two in church tomorrow. Love you." She called over her shoulder.

CHAPTER TEN

"Truly, I tell you, this poor widow has put more into the treasury than all the others."

JESUS CHRIST, "GOSPEL OF JOHN"

Sunday was the only day that the guys did not get to see the girls. That is except from across the small church that encompassed the famous pillar on which the Virgin Mary stood in 40 AD when she appeared to the beleaguered St. James, who was trying to convert the pagans of the area. Even peering at each other from across the church was dangerous as it often resulted in a sharp rebuke from the offender's parents.

God created Sundays for worship and family. Both Ferdinand and Diego were blessed with great families. Diego's family consisted of his mom, Carolina, his father, Diego Sr, and a little sister two years younger than him named Antonella. Ferdinand's mom and dad were Juan and Maria, and he had a little sister the same age as Diego's sister, who everyone referred to as Sis or Sissy, although her given name was Teresa.

Besides being neighbors and good friends, the two families had other things in common as well. Both families were native to Zaragoza and made their living as small business owners. They were also devout Catholics who put family first and held the same values, emphasizing hard work, friendship and education.

One of the main differences between the two families was that while both families were devout Catholics with a strong love for Mary and attended mass regularly, Ferdinand and his family tended to follow the Church's directive and its priests without questions. However, as a result of the Spanish Inquisition and other questionable practices of the time, Diego's father was a little more skeptical.This was especially true of things proclaimed at the local level. One such practice which the Ramirez family took exception was the local church publicly displaying each family's amount that they placed in the collection basket on Sunday.

On more than one occasion, Diego's father met with Fr. Alberta to discuss this practice and present his view that the practice embarrassed the less fortunate parishioners that had a hard time providing food for the family. He reminded the priest of Jesus' parable about the woman and the two copper coins.

However, Fr. Alberta did not feel that, as the parish priest, he should have to consider a simple layperson's position, and he did not appreciate him talking to him about one of Jesus' teachings. As a result, Fr. Alberta refused to discontinue his practice, and Diego Sr. declined to include the family name with his weekly donation.

When Fr. Albert started displaying the list with the assumption that the anonymous donations were that of the Ramirez, the response was young Diego's idea. The family took their regular weekly donation and divided it into six separate contributions, each with a different parishioner's name on it. When Fr. Alberta sat down to put together the list for the following Sunday, he discovered that he had two separate donations from six families and had no way of knowing which amount was from each.

When other families heard about what Diego Sr. had done, they admired him for it because they also disagreed with the practice. Before long, many people copied his example, making it impossible for Fr. Alberta to continue to post his list.

While this was the most widely known of the many disagreements between the local priest and the Ramirez family, it was probably the least significant. Many other disputes focused on the local priest's reluctance to take a stance on several of the day's social issues, such as slavery, and his support for selling indulgences and high positions in the church. All of the problems added up to hostility between the two that was palatable. It even reached a point that if both Diego's family and Ferdinand's family happened to enter the church simultaneously, Fr. Alberta would warmly greet one family while completely ignoring the other. Afterward, both boys would laugh at the absurdity of the situation.

On that particular Sunday, the day after Rosalie's big reveal, Ferdinand and his family ran late, so Diego and his family went on ahead. As he genuflected, Diego looked around the small church for Rosalie and her family. He spied her in their usual spot on the opposite side of the little church with Isabelle and her family seated in the pew behind.

A small raucous from the back of the church signaled to Diego that Ferdinand and his family had arrived and were being greeted by Fr. Alberta. He turned around and watched the Flores walk up the aisle to the pew behind them. Diego looked back at Ferdinand as he entered the bench. "We are okay," he whispered as mass was about to begin.

Ferdinand simply crossed himself and joined in the processional hymn.

CHAPTER ELEVEN

"In true love, the smallest distance is too great, and the greatest distance can be bridged."

HANS NOUWENS

Ferdinand had a difficult time concentrating on mass. It wasn't because the words were in Latin; as the school's best student, he was adept at translating the ancient language. The distraction was due to his mind wandering to Diego, and his encouraging words whispered to him before mass. He felt deep sorrow for his friend because he knew that if Isabelle were moving away, he would not be okay. As his mind wandered, he casually looked over to the girls on the other side of the church, and he wondered how Isabelle was today.

Although the previous night, Isabelle had tried to be brave for her friends' sake, after they had left Diego and Rosalie on the bridge, she cried hard as Ferdinand held her tight. Although the thought of Rosalie moving to Tudela was difficult for Ferdinand too, he understood that Rosalie and Isabelle had been best friends as long as he and Diego had. He could not imagine the pain she was going through as he held her and comforted her as best he could. She still appeared to be somewhat disheveled.

The mass seemed interminable. When it did end, at last, the congregation processed orderly out of the pews and headed for the exits at the back of the church. The four friends searched the crowd of people for each other. Usually, the parents would horde the children to their own home quickly to begin family time but knowing the kids' trauma last night, they gathered together to visit, allowing them time to talk.

After finding each other, immediately Rosalie and Diego fell into each other's arms, while Ferdinand and Isabelle stood side by side quizzically looking at their friends. "How are you two doing?" asked Isabelle, breaking the silence.

"We are fine," said Rosalie, smiling at Diego, "and we want you two to be fine also. After you two left us last night, we talked and cried for a long time. Finally, we came to two conclusions. The first is that our love is not fragile. It is stronger than the distance that might, for a while, divide us. After all, Tudela is only a day's journey away. Secondly, we were not going to waste a single moment that we have left of this summer. The two of us do not have all the answers figured out yet, but regardless we will be together sometime, somewhere. We belong together, and together we will be."

The four friends hugged their good-byes as each headed off with his or her family, feeling better and hopeful for their future.

CHAPTER TWELVE

"Among my stillness was a pounding heart."

SHANNON A. THOMPSON

Diego and Rosalie were true to their word and made every effort to make the following days and weeks memorable for each other and Diego and Rosalie. They didn't mention Rosalie's move at the end of the summer, except to talk about how they would still keep their relationship healthy and swear that the distance between them would not stifle their love. If anything, it would only make it stronger.

Theirs was not a naive determination. They were well aware of the difficulties that a long-distance relationship presented. They knew that they would have to endure periods of loneliness and that constant communication would be necessary to make their relationship work. They would have to save their money to visit each other whenever possible, and Diego would have to work hard and figure out a way to join her in starting their own family as soon as possible.

Fortunately, they would have a lot of support. Besides their two friends who would do anything for them, they had supportive families behind them. Diego's parents were extremely fond of Rosalie, and Rosalie's parents felt the same way about Diego. Both families cherished the idea of their children getting together and were even more enthusiastic about the possibility of being grandparents someday.

As the days and the weeks passed, the four friends spent much time together. However, after Rosalie's announcement, one change that did occur was that they also spent more time together as couples instead of as a foursome. This suited Isabelle and Ferdinand well. Not only did they understand the need for Diego and Rosalie to have alone time, but they also treasured their time by themselves greatly.

Their relationship with each other was somewhat typical of young couples of their time, with one significant difference. Ferdinand's life was so anchored in his faith and his love for Jesus and his Mother that, as Isabelle was drawn closer to Ferdinand, she couldn't help but be pulled closer to that which made him so unique and, in her eyes, special.

Besides openly sharing their dreams and feelings for each other, the couple spent many hours together talking about Jesus, Mary the Lady of the Pillar, and the saints. Isabelle had always been amazed that the Mother of God had appeared to St. James in her own town. Even though the event occurred almost fifteen hundred years earlier, she still thought that it made them all special. All of her life, she knew of the apparition, and that the town depended largely on devout Catholics making a pilgrimage to the pillar that was located within the walls of their tiny church. Still, somehow her relationship with Diego made her have a closer devotion to Mary as well.

Every year, Fr. Alberta would push the people and the government for funds to create a more fitting monument to the Lady of the Pillar than the simple church that currently constituted her home. It greatly distressed him that the town's principal cathedral was a magnificent tribute to St Mary Magdalen when its central claim to fame was Mary's apparition.

However, while most agreed that the Lady of the Pillar deserved a much more fitting tribute than the small church provided, it was unlikely that the funds necessary or the desire to build a glorious cathedral would happen in the near future.

King Ferdinand and Queen Isabella had only united the country less than fifty years earlier. They and their successors were consumed with many other projects, including strengthening their hold on the country and their role in the ill-conceived Spanish Inquisition. However, the most crucial reason was Spain's obsession with amassing a great fortune through exploration and conquering foreign lands.

In their conversations, Ferdinand and Isabelle agreed that Fr. Alberta's drive for the cathedral probably had more to do with his wanting to be the pastor of the most beautiful cathedral in Spain than a desire to honor Mary. They both loved their cozy little church. They felt comfortable there and were convinced that Mary of the Pillar did too.

Isabelle knew that she was falling deeper and deeper in love with Ferdinand. Oddly enough, it was during their discussions on faith that she felt the closest to him. One afternoon, as she and Ferdinand lay on a hillside overlooking the town, watching the clouds roll across the mostly blue sky, she decided to broach the subject that had been on her mind for some time. She felt her stomach tie up in knots, and she turned on her side and, laying her head on Ferdinand's chest, said, "Ferdinand, I have something to tell you."

Now Ferdinand's stomach began to knot up. "Isabelle, you know you can tell me anything. You know that I love you."

"I know that you love me, and you know that I love you too," said Isabelle quietly, "But what are we doing? I mean, on that last day of school when Rosalie and I let you guys know that we were interested in taking our friendship to the next level, I didn't know how much I was going to fall in love with you. I knew that you were contemplating a life in the priesthood, but I thought that we could have fun as a couple before you did, and I very much wanted my first boyfriend to be you. But I didn't know that I could fall in love so hard so quickly."

"I guess what I am saying is that I want you to know that I would fight to my last breath not to lose you to another girl," she said, wiping away tears, "but I will not stand in your way if you were to choose God and our Mother over me. I mean, it will hurt, but for you, I will endure the pain. You are the best man that I have ever known, and I want you to know that if you feel it is God's will for you to be a priest, then it is my will too. If you feel we need some time apart for you to think about and pray about things, I will give you as much time and space as you need."

Ferdinand held Isabelle tightly and wiped away her tears. "I do not need time or space to discern what I should do," he said. "I love you and always will. I, too, did not know that a person could fall in love so deeply and so quickly. When we first started going out, I also thought that we could have a great summer before entering the seminary, but my feelings for you have changed everything. The reason that I don't need time and space is that I have already been praying and thinking about us for several weeks."

"I know that it was God that drew us together, and that God did it for a reason," he explained. "Of all of the blessings in my life, you are the one about which I am certain was ordained by God. We are meant for each other. As I prayed about us, it came to me that I most wanted to be a priest because I wanted to spend my life helping people, as Jesus did. I now know that I don't have to be a priest to do that. We can do that together."

"My dream, Isabelle," he said now crying himself, " is to ask you to marry me when the time is right. To love, Jesus, Mary, and you forever. To raise children with you and do good for others. I want to teach our children to love and serve God and others too. Please, please, don't ever think about leaving me."

"As Our Lady of the Pillar as my witness," she said, "I will always be with you."

The two lay together quietly, watching the clouds float across the sky. Neither of them spoke. They were happy, peaceful, and in love. They continued to watch until they both fell asleep in each other's arms. Neither of them could have known that within days their dreams and their entire world would be turned inside out. .

CHAPTER THIRTEEN

"Sometimes one feels suddenly doomed by fate."

IRIS MURDOCH

It was Tuesday morning when Ferdinand helped set out the breakfast plates. As he worked, his mind went back to a conversation that his father had with him several years ago. Mr. Flores had been sharing with him the story about when his father had died. He said that as he closed the restaurant that night, he couldn't stop the feeling that something was wrong. He had no idea what was wrong or with whom something was wrong, but something was not as it should be in his world, and he could not figure out what it was.

He finished his work and hurried home as fast as he could. As he entered the door, he called for his wife and children. All responded, and all were okay. That night he was restless in bed and slept only intermittently. No matter what he did, he could not shake his ominous feeling. Finally, that morning, he was awakened by a knock on the door and the news that his father had passed the evening before.

Ferdinand had not thought of that story until that morning when it burdened him much, because as he worked, the same feeling that his father had described haunted him. He tried to lose himself in his work, but no matter what he did, the feeling seemed to be right around the corner, nagging at his psyche. He tried to tell himself that he was just upset by Rosalie's leaving next month, but without knowing how he knew, he knew that wasn't it.

Finally, the cafe's lunch hour was over, and it was time for Ferdinand to meet Diego on the bridge. Ferdinand hurried off, hoping to get assurances that his fears were unfounded. Isabelle had been optimistic that she would be able to join the boys for lunch because her mother was going in the afternoon to visit her sister, Isabelle's favorite aunt. He knew if something were wrong with his mom or his sister at home, a neighbor would have sent word to his father. So if he met Diego and Isabelle for lunch, and they were okay, it would only leave Rosalie, and there would be a good chance that Isabelle would have stopped in on her en route to the bridge. As he approached the bridge, he saw Diego sitting as he always sat with his legs dangling over the bridge like a little kid. Ferdinand could also see a girl nearing from the opposite side but soon recognized the form not to be Isabelle but Rosalie.

When he arrived, Diego and Rosalie greeted him, but his mind was too preoccupied to answer. "Where is Isabelle?" Ferdinand asked Rosalie.

"I was just about to ask you the same thing," replied Rosalie uneasily. "I didn't stop by, because I figured that she would be here already."

Ferdinand quickly shared his fears with Diego and Rosalie. He excused himself to run off and check on Isabelle, but Diego and Rosalie rose to join him. The three walked quickly, as Diego was hopeful that they could put his friend's mind at ease and get back to work before his allotted lunchtime was over. Before they got to the door, they knew something was terribly wrong.

Isabelle's mom was not at her sister's house. Isabelle's aunt was standing in the front garden with her mom, and both women were violently crying. It was the aunt that approached the gate when they saw the friends coming. It was apparent that her mom could not compose herself enough to speak with them. "The doctor just left." she said quietly." Isabelle has consumption. It came on quickly late last night. The doctor said he had never known consumption to grab a hold on someone so fast, and he gave her something to help keep her quiet and the fever down while her body fights to recover. She is young and strong. There is nothing that anyone can do for her now except pray."

She turned to return to her sister, leaving the three friends staring at each other stunned.

CHAPTER FOURTEEN

> *"You never know how strong you are...until being strong is the only choice you have."*
>
> ANONYMOUS

The next morning, Ferdinand stopped by to check on Isabelle on his way to the restaurant. Mr. Flores had assured Ferdinand that he did not need to go to work, but Ferdinand knew that the battle against consumption was typically a long one. It generally took weeks for people to overcome or succumb to its effects. Ferdinand knew that he would not be allowed to see Isabelle until the fever had subsided for at least twenty-four hours, and just hanging around his house worrying would drive him crazy.

Before leaving each other the night before, Diego, Rosalie, and Ferdinand agreed how to support Isabelle until they could again be with her. Ferdinand would get an update on his way to work and share his findings with his friends at lunch. After dinner, Rosalie would stop by Isabelle's house for a second update, which she would share with her friends at the church where they would gather to pray the rosary asking Mary, the Lady of the Pillar's help.

Mrs. Lopez was out hanging sheets when Ferdinand arrived. She walked over to meet him at the gate. "I had to change sheets again. The fever has Isabelle sweating and shaking terribly. The medicine and cold cloths bring it down for a little while, but then it returns. The doctor is coming by again today after he has had a chance to do some research and talk to neighboring doctors to see what is going on."

"Does she know what is happening?" asked Ferdinand.

"During the times that she is not shaking with the fever, she falls into an exhausted state of sleep. During her few lucid moments when she is awake, she vows that she will 'beat this thing.' She says how much she loves us, Rosalie, Diego, and especially you, Ferdinand. She says to keep you away from her. She worries that someone else may get sick because of her. She says that she knows that you all are praying for her. She asks that you keep praying, and she will keep fighting."

"Typical Isabelle, she is stricken with a horrible disease, and even while she is fighting for her life, she is thinking about others. You and Isabelle's father have done an amazing job." Ferdinand sobbed.

Mrs. Lopez responded by reaching over the short garden wall and embracing Ferdinand in a warm hug. Ferdinand assured her of all of their prayers, turned, and headed to work.

CHAPTER FIFTEEN

"All things are difficult before they are easy."

THOMAS FULLER

After dinner, Ferdinand and Diego walked to the church to wait for Rosalie's update and join in prayer for their sick friend. As Diego opened the door to allow Ferdinand to enter first, they saw Rosalie running down the street. She gasped for her breath as she approached the boys.

"As I arrived, the doctor was just leaving," she said, fighting for air. Mr. and Mrs. Lopez said it was okay for me to hear what he had to say. The doctor said that he was sure that Isabelle has the consumption, but there has to be something else that is making the disease, which is horrible by itself, act more quickly than it usually would. They do not precisely know what it is. They said it could be something that she has had from birth, but they did not know about it. There is no way of knowing."

"But she will get better?" Ferdinand blurted in a panic.

"They don't know," said Rosalie, who wanted to be reassuring but was unwilling to lie to her friend. "They said that the next twenty-four hours would be crucial. If only she can hang on until morning, she has a fairly good chance of recovery."

Without a word, Ferdinand turned and headed down the

church's steps to the street. Rosalie and Diego ran to catch up. "Where are you going?" asked Diego. "We know you are upset, so are we. That is why we need to go in and pray."

"I need to be closer. I need to be as close to her as I can be," Said Ferdinand holding on to Diego's shoulders and looking him in the eyes.

Diego nodded his understanding, and the three friends headed off hand-in-hand-in-hand to Isabelle's house, stopping immediately outside of the garden gate. They took positions sitting against the garden wall, and each pulled out their rosaries and started to pray.

Several hours later, three women approached them. The friends prepared to present to their mothers why they could not go home for the night. But instead of ordering their children home, the three mothers pulled out blankets from a bag each carried and spread it on the ground; then, sitting, they joined their son and daughters in prayer. After finishing a rosary, the mothers stood and hugged each of the children. "We will be praying at home, and so will your fathers," they said before heading down the road.

Ather the moms had left, Ferdinand suggested that they each take turns praying to Mary of the Pillar while the other two rested. That way, there would be an unceasing stream of prayers asking for Mary's intercession. "Pray as you have never prayed in your lives," implored Ferdinand.

Ferdinand prayed the first rosary, followed by Rosalie and lastly Diego. They frantically repeated the process throughout the night and into the early morning hours. Suddenly, at the same time, the three smelled a beautiful and robust fragrance. They were overcome by a sense of peace that they had never experienced and which words could not express. Then the aroma vanished as quickly as it came.

Without a word, each picked up their blankets and walked silently back to their own homes. They could not have explained their experience or what they were feeling, even if they had tried, but somehow all three knew exactly what it meant.

CHAPTER SIXTEEN

"I will not say: do not weep, for all tears are not an evil."

J.R.R. TOLKEIN, THE RETURN OF THE KING

After a very short but deep sleep, Ferdinand woke up to knocking on the door. He walked into the kitchen as his mother was opening the door for Diego and Rosalie. The troubled look on their faces said everything that could be said. When Ferdinand saw them, his legs buckled from under him, and he would have fallen to the floor if Diego had not caught him. With Rosalie's help, they managed to get him to a chair.

"Mrs. Lopez said that she passed peacefully early this morning," said Rosalie after Ferdinand had gained a little bit of composure. "She came out to tell us, but as she did, she saw us get up and head home. She somehow knew that we already knew. I dropped by this morning to confirm what we all felt last night. She did give me a letter that Isabelle wrote to all of us. She has no idea how or when she would have written it."

My Dearest Ferdinand, Rosalie, and Diego,

Ever since this terrible disease attacked me, I have been trying to find a way to write this letter to you so that if I did not survive,

I could leave you with a testament to the love I have for all of you. Every time the fever subsided and I went to write, sleep overtook me, and I could not do so. Then the fever was back. It continued this way for two days, then this evening, right after dinner, it all changed. I was in the throes of the fever when I heard someone in the other room say, "Isabelle's friends are out front saying prayers." A short time later, the fever left me for good. As I write this letter to you, I feel an inexplicable sense of peace, and my thoughts are clearer than they have ever been in my life. I am in the care of our Mother and am experiencing deep joy. I have no concerns for myself. My only sadness comes from leaving you all behind, but even that sadness is tempered by the knowledge that you are also in good hands, and our separation will not be forever.

Rosalie, my dear sister, some people spend an entire life and never find a friend as wonderful as you, and we found each other when we were only three. Do you remember the day that our moms were talking in the other room when we decided it would be a good idea to cut each other's hair? We thought that they would be so pleased that we saved them the money it would cost for a haircut that they would take us out for sweets. We didn't get the outcome we were hoping we would.

Rosalie, I want to thank you for being my everything, but somehow thank you doesn't seem enough. It is beyond the power of words to describe how wonderful it has been all of my life to have someone with whom I could tell everything and with whom I could share everything. Nothing was out of bounds. We shared everything, the awkwardness of growing into womanhood, experimenting with different hairstyles, drinking our first bottle of wine, which we snuck from your dad's collection, and even plotting how we were going to get Ferdinand and Diego to realize that we liked them also. What an experience it has been, my sister. I love you dearly, and I always will.

Diego, what can I say to you. You have always been a dear friend to me. I could not be happier for you and Rosalie for having found each other. Watching you two fall in love has been an absolute joy. I care for both of you so deeply, I know that most people see you as an outgoing and athletic person, but I have gotten to know a different side of you. Besides being outgoing and athletic, you are also very intelligent, gentle, and unbelievably loyal. All the beautiful qualities that the man who is to marry my sister will need. Please know that on the day that you and Rosalie wed, I will be there in a genuine way.

Finally, to you, the love of my life and my soulmate, Ferdinand. Words cannot even come close to expressing the enormity of my love for you. That is why, so often, when we were together, we didn't need to say anything. We simply enjoyed being in each other's love.

You have given me more than you will ever know. Please know that while I am happy, at peace, and in good hands, it is in no way my decision to leave you, but you are the reason that I am okay. Because of you, Ferdinand, I do not leave the world without knowing the true love of a good man, but more than that, my faith is strong, and I am ready to meet Jesus and our Mother. I am a better woman because of your love for me. I would have loved to have been able to live our love as husband and wife and to create new life out of our love, but that is not to be. I do not know why. There is one thing that I know for sure, and that is that in our brief time together, we shared more love than many couples do in years.

I would tell you, my love, not to grieve for me, but I know that would be like telling the sun not to shine or the birds not to sing. So grieve if you must, but please try not to suffer too long. Let Rosalie and Diego help you, as I know that you will be there for them. Let go of the pain of our loss as quickly as possible, but always remember our love, and know that it will never end. It will always be there.

I don't know what our Lord and His Mother have planned for your life, but please, know that it will be unique and full of love and joy. If your mission is to serve others as a priest, you will know it when the time comes. I know that you were right when you discerned that in whatever way you are to live, your life is meant to be lived helping others.

Finally, Ferdinand, this might be hard for you to hear right now, but I must say it. If falling in love with someone in the future, someone to join you in helping others is meant for you, please know that you have my blessing and more -- I will be very happy for you. I now know that love is not something that people have in limited quantity. The more love you give, the more love you have to offer. If you are meant to love another woman, it will in no way lessen your love for me or my love for you. If anything, it will increase your capacity to love me and others. I will never forget the first time I grabbed your hand and felt your hand in mine. I somehow knew in my heart that we were embarking on something special. Talk to me if you like. I may not be able to answer in a traditional way, but I will always be there for you, and I will always love you. Be open to my prompting and the prompting of our Mother. I promise I will never really leave you.

Love always,

Isabelle

PART TWO

CHAPTER SEVENTEEN

"The darker the night, the brighter the stars, The deeper the grief, the closer is God!

FYODOR DOSTOEVSKY

For the next couple of weeks, Ferdinand felt as if he were living his life in a fog. Even the simplest tasks, such as getting dressed or eating breakfast, took what seemed like a heroic effort on his part. His only motivation was the final words that Isabelle had imparted to him and his friends in her letter. He could not disappoint her.

He frequently talked to her as she suggested in her farewell. Sometimes he could feel her close; many times, he could not, but he believed. As he climbed the stairs to the church for her funeral, it felt like he was wearing heavy boots and walking through deep mud.

As the whole parish mourned Isabelle's death at the cemetery, Ferdinand felt as if he lived outside his own body. He, Diego, and Rosalie all held each other wordlessly. At some level, each of them knew that they were not only saying goodbye to a beloved friend but also something else — they were saying goodbye to the carefree days of summer; and more. They were saying goodbye to their childhoods.

CHAPTER EIGHTEEN

"Those we love don't go away. They walk beside us every day."

ANONYMOUS

The three friends had two weeks after Isabelle's funeral before Rosalie, and her family was scheduled to move. During that time, they spent as much time as they could together, helping each other with the grieving process. They would talk for hours, recounting fun times that they shared. But for the first time in his life, Ferdinand began to feel something that he had never felt around his friends; he felt a little bit awkward.

He knew that Diego and Rosalie loved him and needed him, just as he loved and needed them. But now, their situation was different. Diego and Rosalie not only loved each other, but they were also in love with each other, as he and Isabelle had been. Now that Isabelle was gone, Ferdinand didn't always know when Diego and Rosalie needed to be with him, and when they needed to be alone together. Eventually, he settled into a routine that he thought would work for all of them.

Both Diego and Ferdinand, along with their families, decided that the boys would not go back to school in the fall. Diego started to work full time with his father and started to save his money to open his store somewhere as soon as possible. Diego and Rosalie were anxious to begin their lives together, and they had an eye on a shoe store that was to become available when Mr. Moralez retired. Mr. Moralez had made overtures to the fact that he would be retiring for the last couple of years, but even he was unsure as to when he actually would. Because the fine leather business, which Mr. Ramirez owned, shared many of the same suppliers as the shoe business, they already had many valuable contacts.

Ferdinand explained to his parents that he needed time to think and discern his future. At Isabelle's wake, Fr. Alberta suggested that now he may want to reconsider entering the seminary. He even went as far as to suggest that Isabelle's death was a sign from God that he should. When Diego heard that the priest made that statement, it took everything that Rosalie could do to prevent him from going after him. Thankfully, Rosalie and Diego were able to assure Ferdinand that God did not work that way, and that his choosing a life of service with Isabelle over the seminary was not why she had died.

While Ferdinand had now lost what little respect he had for Fr. Alberta, he knew many other priests who were good and righteous, and he was mature enough not to judge them all by one person's actions. Perhaps he was being called into the priesthood. All that he knew at the moment was that which Isabelle had written; however he was to live his life, his mission was to help people. How he was to do it was yet for him to determine.

Always the practical one, Ferdinand devised a plan to discern his path. He would pray to the Lady of the Pillar and her Son, and he would help people. He would also ask Isabelle, who he knew in his heart was with them in heaven, to intercede on his behalf and give him a sign. He had faith that when the time was right, he would know.

The timing was fortunate in that Ferdinand's father's assistant decided to take another job, leaving a full-time position open that he could fill. Ferdinand felt that the best place to start helping people was at home. He needed very little money for himself, as his expenses were few. He planned to give half of the money that he earned to the town orphanage and save the other half for Diego and Rosalie to start their lives together. Ferdinand kept that latter part of the plan to himself, because he wanted it to surprise his friends. He also anticipated both of them arguing against such a sacrifice. The truth was that he could not think of anything that would make him happier than helping his friends start their lives as man and wife.

Ferdinand quickly fell into a routine that allowed him time to help others, spend time with his friends, and let Diego and Rosalie have time alone. He would rise early and go to church and pray the rosary. He would then go to work. At lunch, he would meet Diego and Rosalie on the bridge. On his way home from work, he would stop by the orphanage and help the children with their homework. Then, after dinner, he would visit Diego and Rosalie. After a few hours, he would excuse himself, leaving the couple some time alone and allowing him to help get the children at the orphanage get ready for bed on his way home.

It was Saturday morning on the day that Rosalie and her family were scheduled to move. The three friends gathered for breakfast. It was a beautiful day, and they chose to eat their breakfasts on the bridge, where they had shared so many meals. When it was over, Ferdinand stood to leave.

"Where are you going?" asked Rosalie, reaching for his arm.

"It's time for me to head to the orphanage to play with the kids, I promised them. Besides, you two need some time together. Come here," he said to Rosalie. She stood and wrapped him in a hug.

"Goodbye, my friend," she said to him.

"Not goodbye," he responded, "It's see you later. You know that you will be back in October for the festival. Please know that my love and prayers are with you."

"You too.' She responded.

He turned around and headed off to leave his two friends to bid each other farewell.

CHAPTER NINETEEN

"Time has a way of showing us what really matters."
Anonymous

October 9, 1526

It was early in the morning when Rosalie boarded the coach headed back to Zaragoza. In a few more hours, she would be back home and in Diego's arms and able to catch up in person with her good friend, Ferdinand.

Time seemed to have stood still, and she couldn't seem to relax for more than a few minutes. As she traveled, her mind went back to another day when time stood still, the last day of term. Momentarily, as she thought of the remarkable stunt that she, Diego, and Isabelle pulled, Rosalie felt a pang of sadness over the loss of her good friend, but suddenly she couldn't stop laughing. She knew it was the laughter and not the sadness that Isabelle would want for her.

As the stagecoach finally pulled into the station, predictably, both Diego and Ferdinand were waiting to greet her. "I missed you, dear brother," said Rosalie as she hugged Ferdinand. "How have you been?" Rosalie knew that Ferdinand was as well as could be expected through her almost daily written correspondence with Diego, but she wanted to hear directly from Ferdinand.

"Better, now that you are here," said Ferdinand. "I still miss her, of course, but every day I am a little less sad. I talk to her often, and I know that she is still with me, with us all, so I carry on."

"I know. I feel her too. I know that she wants us all to be happy," she said, giving Ferdinand one more squeeze before falling into Diego's arms.

"My love, I cannot thank you enough for all the letters. They make my days brighter and continue to give me hope for our lives together. However, nothing compares to being in your arms."

"Yada, yada, yada," joked Ferdinand as he put Rosalie's bag in the back of the wagon and climbed up in it with them. "Come join me when you two lovebirds are ready, so we can let Rosalie settle in at her aunt's house. Mom and Dad are expecting both of you for dinner tonight if it works for you?"

"Works for me," replied Rosalie.

"Me too, especially since I smelled your mom's apple pie wafting out the window this morning," added Diego as he wrapped his arm over Rosalie's shoulders, and the two sauntered over to the wagon.

CHAPTER TWENTY

"Getting over a painful experience is much like crossing monkey bars. You have to let go at some point in order to move forward.

C.S. LEWIS

After the meal was over and everyone had seconds of Mrs. Flores' apple pie, Diego, Rosalie, and Ferdinand walked to town. As they approached the outskirts of the city, Diego said, "Come with me Rosalie, I have something to show you." Taking a right on Second Street, the three stopped in front of Mr. Guiseppe's Fine Leather Shoes. "This is it," said Diego proudly. "The future home of Rosalie and Diego's Fine Leather Shoes. And that is not all. There are living quarters upstairs where we can stay once we are married. I mean, not for long. Once we get married and the business going strong, we will move into our own house. It is not the home that I want to give you, Rosalie, but as we are just."

Rosalie interrupted him. "The store is wonderful," she said, "and you are my home. I don't care where we live. I don't care if it is above the store, or in a house, or wherever. If I am with you, I am home.``

"I am not sure when Mr. Guiseppe will finally retire, but I will work as hard as I can so that I can make him an offer when the time comes. Mom and Dad said that they might be able to loan me some of the money as well," said Diego.

As they continued on their way, Ferdinand spoke up. "You know, of course, that I love reading about the saints and that Isabelle and I talked about all kinds of things, Jesus, Mary, faith, and the Saints." Rosalie and Diego nodded knowingly. Ferdinand continued, " Not only about that, of course, but we also talked about all kinds of things. We talked about you guys and what a great couple you are."

"Go on." replied Diego, "but first, tell us why you seem nervous. You know that we are your best friends and would do anything for you. You can tell us or ask us anything."

"Good, remember that," said Ferdinand as he pushed on with what he was saying. "Well, one of the women who Isabelle had heard about is a woman named Angela Merici who, along with her company of women, teach young girls in the town of Brescia, Italy. She said many wise things that she wrote down as counsel to her followers. Both Isabelle and I loved many of them, but our favorite was, "You have a greater need to serve others than they have of being served by you."

Now Diego and Rosalie stopped and looked at him, anticipating that he had some point which he was going to make. "Well," he said. "Ever since I have been working full time, I have spent my earnings in two ways. I have given almost half of them to the kids at the orphanage, and I have saved the other half for my two best friends as you prepare to start your life together. I want to continue to do so. Isabelle, I know, wants me to do so. For my sake, I mean for our sake, mine and Isabelle, please don't fight me on this."

Rosalie and Diego were stunned. After a few moments of awkward silence, they embraced Ferdinand in a three-way hug. "Thank you! We won't fight you on this," said Diego, "but are you sure that when we can, you don't want us to pay the money back."

"No," replied Ferdinand. "If at some point things are going very well for you and you are in the position where you could pay it back, I want you to pay it forward if that is what you want to do. Give it to the orphanage or some worthy cause in Isabelle's name."

Diego and Isabelle were speechless. The three friends quietly walked the rest of the way, stopping only once for Ferdinand to read a notice posted to a wall outside of town.

CHAPTER TWENTY-ONE

"If you were going to be successful in the world of crime, you needed a reputation for honesty."

TERRY PRATCHETT

The next day, Diego, Rosalie, and Ferdinand met at their usual spot on the bridge for lunch. However, they did meet a little later than usual because the town festival provided a brisk business for both the leather shop and restaurant, making it harder for the boys to leave.

"I have always loved this festival, ever since I was a little girl. Our moms would always bring Isabelle and me every year until we were old enough to go on our own. I remember the excitement as the event approached. It was almost like a small Christmas for us," said Rosalie.. "Of course, my favorite part was always the evening of 12 October with those beautiful fireworks. I think it is so wonderful that the festival celebrating Our Lady of the Pillar coincides with the day that Christopher Columbus, our national hero, discovered America."

"Oh no!" groaned Ferdinand, "Please tell me that she didn't just go there."

"Go where?" asked Rosalie, confused. But before Ferdinand could answer, Diego started in.

"Christopher Columbus is no national hero of Spain," he began.

"And we're there!' exclaimed Ferdinand as he got up and picked up an imaginary item. "Your soapbox, my friend, if you are going to enlighten the good lady, you might as well have the proper soapbox."

"I take it that you don't agree with Diego on that which he is about to espouse?" Rosalie mused.

"On the contrary. I agree with him. I am just giving him trouble because, one, I have heard this pronouncement so many times already; I can't believe that you haven't. Two, it is so much fun to give him trouble," said Ferdinand smiling.

Rosalie, in turn, gave him a playful punch to his shoulder. "Go, ahead," said Ferdinand, turning to Diego, "Enlighten the lady."

"Well, now that you two are finally done!" began Diego feigning frustration. "As I was saying, how can Columbus be our national hero? Don't you think that Spain's national hero should be Spanish? I know he became a Spanish citizen and even died in Seville a few years back, but that doesn't make him Spanish. He only came to Spain because he needed backing for his idea to travel to the east by going west. His own country was in no position to help him, so he came to King Ferdinand and Queen Isabella, but we weren't even his first choice. First, he went to the Portuguese, but they had invested too heavily in reaching Asia by sailing around Africa. They didn't feel that it would be prudent to change their strategy to do so. So he came to Spain as a last resort. Yes, Spain has gained much because of his bold exploration, but he didn't do it selflessly. He drove a hard bargain and negotiated a very lucrative deal for himself. So no, I do not consider Christopher Columbus to be a national hero."

"The man does make some good points," said Rosalie, smiling at Ferdinand.

"Oh, he's not done," responded Ferdinand rolling his eyes. Both of them turned back to Diego, "Continue," encouraged Ferdinand.

Diego cleared his throat, "As I was saying, Columbus negotiated an astronomical deal with our King and Queen to chart a new water passage to Asia. Not only did he not do that even after four tries, but he also wasn't even astute enough to know that he did not do it. It was only after Amerigo Vespucci's voyages and calculations that the world realized that the land that Columbus so called discovered was land unknown to us before his travels. Don't get me wrong, I believe Christopher Columbus was courageous, and his voyages changed much in the world today, but he was neither a saint nor a national hero. I could go on all day."

"He literally could," said Ferdinand nodding to Rosalie, "But alas, we both must get back to work, duty calls." He said as he stood gathering his things. After bidding Rosalie farewell and promising that they would see her after work, the two started back to their respective shops.

CHAPTER TWENTY-TWO

"God has given us two hands. One to receive and one to give with."

BILLY GRAHAM

After work that evening, the two boys met Rosalie on the bridge and headed to the orphanage together. Ever since Rosalie moved out of town, Diego had joined Ferdinand in his daily visits to the orphanage. In his many letters to Rosalie, Diego shared his experiences with the orphans with her. He told her how much he loved the kids and how much working with them had helped him with missing her. She was anxious to join the boys with their visits. After dinner that night was going to be very special, because they would be able to take the children to the festival.

As soon as the kids saw Ferdinand and Diego, they attacked, hugging and chattering at the same time. "Is it time for us to go? When are we going?"

"We ah not going to go until after dinna," said Maria, a curly-headed five-year-old with big dark eyes who could not pronounce her 'r's. Then spying Rosalie, she added, "Is this your girlfriend, Mista. Diego? She's pretty. Are you going to mawwy him?" she asked, tugging on Rosalie's hand.

"Well, we are not engaged yet, but I certainly hope so." smiled Rosalie.

"Well, he's okay, but I am going to mawwy Mr. Ferdinand," she announced. All three of them laughed as Ferdinand lifted Maria and threw her up in the air.

Ferdinand, Diego, and Rosalie had difficulty getting the kids to concentrate on their studies because they were so excited about the festival. While Rosalie worked with Maria, she kept looking at Diego out of the corner of her eye.

As if reading her thoughts, Ferdinand reached over and whispered in her ear, "He will make a fantastic father someday." Rosalie smiled, "And you, my dear friend," he added, "Will make a marvelous mother."

Rosalie again smiled, thinking how much she loved Ferdinand, and she knew he loved her too. Of course, it was not the same love that she had for Diego, that was different, but the love was real and strong. She realized that she didn't know if she could have gotten over the loss of Isabelle without Ferdinand and Diego.

On the way to dinner, Ferdinand stopped by the same sign that he had the night before. "What are you thinking?" asked Diego as Ferdinand rejoined Rosalie and him.

"Oh, it's just an advertisement for people to join a restocking mission to New Spain," he said. "Just thinking," he added, "Not seriously at this point. Just messing with the idea."

Diego and Rosalie glanced at each other, with nervous looks on their faces, but said nothing.

CHAPTER TWENTY-THREE

"Adventure is worthwhile in itself."

AMELIA EARHART

"Do you think he is serious?" asked Rosalie nervously as she and Diego read the pamphlet together.

Ready for Adventure?

Want to Make a Year's Salary in Less than Four Months?

Want to Explore New Lands for God and Spain?

Inquire at #5 Paseo Teruel. No Experience Necessary.

I don't know," responded Diego. "It certainly doesn't seem like him. He has never said anything about wanting to go exploring and knows nothing about sailing."

"I guess that we will find out soon enough," said Rosalie as she nodded toward Ferdinand, who was approaching the bridge where they were to meet and eat."

After exchanging their hellos, Ferdinand began, "Well, I saw you two looking at the poster."

"Yes, said Rosalie. "We were wondering what had grabbed your attention. You aren't seriously thinking about signing on! Are you?"

"No, not thinking about it," responded Ferdinand. "I did yesterday evening."

Both Diego and Rosalie stared at him in total disbelief. "But, why?" asked Diego. "You have never shown even the slightest interest in joining the exploration of the New World in the past? What has changed? Money, adventure, fame, none of that has ever meant much to you! Are you sure that with dealing with Isabelle's death and Rosalie's moving and all, that this is the right time for you to make such a monumental decision?"

"Don't you see? Isabelle's dying and Rosalie's moving are precisely the right reasons for me to do this. In my life right now, I am sure of only a few things. I know that my future and the key for me to understand my life lies in helping others. Another is that both Isabelle and I want you two to be together forever as man and wife as soon as possible. I cannot be with Isabelle for reasons that I will never understand, at least while I am living here on earth, but you two are meant to have what we could not. We don't envy you. It makes us happy. I am positive that Isabelle would tell you the same thing if she were physically here."

"Please don't try to talk me out of this. I know it is sudden, but I have prayed to Jesus, His mother, and Isabelle, and I am convinced that this is the right thing for me to do. The money could help get you two set up, and I could use a change right now. I checked, and it is just a restocking mission more than an exploration. The ship is scheduled to sail to New Spain, deliver fresh horses and supplies, and pick up goods to carry back here. With the new ships being lighter and much faster, it should only take us about a month and a half to reach the Americas. We will spend two weeks there loading up and preparing for our return trip, and off we sail back home. Of course, nothing is exact and much depends on the weather."

"Are you sure, Ferdinand?" asked Rosalie as her lower lip began to quiver. "The thought of you being so far away scares me, and if something were to happen to you too, well. .."

Ferdinand interrupted, "Nothing is going to happen to me. I can take care of myself. Besides, I already signed up and accepted the signing bonus. It is too late for me to turn back now even if I wanted to do so."

"But you know nothing about sailing," interjected Diego. "Why would they hire you? What type of work will you be doing?"

"There is such a push to get people to settle in New Spain and to conquer new territories for God and country that they are looking for whatever help they can find. Specifically, I will be working below deck with the horses that they are transporting and helping out the ship's cook."

"What did your parents say about your plan?" asked Diego.

"I can't honestly say that they were thrilled, but they understand. Mom and Dad know that helping people, especially you two, is important to me, and they support that. You know that both of you are like family to them too, don't you? They also know that the time on the ocean will give me some valuable time to pray and to discern my life."

"I don't know what to say," said Diego quietly.

"Me either," offered Rosalie looking first into Ferdinand's eyes and then into Diego's. "How did I ever get so blessed?" she said, tears flowing down her cheeks.

Two nights later, Diego walked Rosalie back to her aunt's house after spending her last day in town with her two friends. Diego was unusually quiet and seemed very nervous. As they approached the house, Rosalie broke the silence. "Well, have you signed up to sail to New Spain yet?"

"No," said Diego, taking Rosalie in her arms, "and if you don't want me to go, I won't."

"Go." Said Rosalie softly. "If I were to ask you not to go, to let Ferdinand make the trip alone, I would be asking you not to be you. I love you for many reasons; not the least is your love and loyalty to your family, Ferdinand and me. So I can't very well ask you not to go, but I will tell you this, mister. When you return, you are going to get me, and we are going to be married, and I don't care if we live above a store, in a closet, or in a crate somewhere. Got it? Any questions?" she asked as she playfully grabbed him by the collar.

"Just one," Diego said as he dropped to one knee and pulled the ring that had once belonged to his grandmother out of his pocket.

CHAPTER TWENTY-FOUR

'For in every adult there dwells the child that was, and ievery child there lies the adult that will be."

JOHN CONNOLLY

The trip from Zaragoza in the northern region of Spain to the port of Palos in the far south was long and arduous. Diego and Ferdinand were glad to have each other's company, or what was a very long trip would have seemed even longer. They spent the time reminiscing about their summer, Isabelle, and all the fun they had growing up. While they enjoyed their strolls down memory lane, there was also a somewhat melancholy feel to their remembrances, not only because of Isabelle, but also because of the loss of something more intangible. Once again, while the two friends prepared to embark on their most incredible adventure together to date, they couldn't help but feel that they were indeed crossing the threshold into adulthood.

After a few days, their conversation shifted from memories of the past to plans for the future. As Ferdinand's fate was still mostly unknown, the discussion naturally focused on Diego and Rosalie's upcoming life. Initially, Diego was a little self-conscious about spending so much time talking about Rosalie and their plans, considering that Ferdinand's dreams of a life with Isabelle were cut short. However, it soon became clear to him that Ferdinand was not only okay with him sharing the couple's dreams, he genuinely loved talking about them. During the conversation, Diego was very moved by the depth of Ferdinand's love for both him and Rosalie.

Finally, after ten days of travel, the coach pulled into the port of Palos, the same port from which Christopher Columbus sailed in 1492 as he set off looking for a water passage to Asia. The hope then, of course, was that the route would not only be shorter but also safer, as travel across the land had become increasingly dangerous after the fall of Constantinople to the Muslims in 1453.

After disembarking from the coach, Diego and Ferdinand followed the directions given them to an old rustic hotel's lobby. Once inside, they saw a sign affixed to a small table that read, "New Spain Voyagers Sign in". After providing the necessary information, they were each given a voucher for dinner in the cafe and a key to the same hotel room. As the man handed them the key, he remarked, "The beds here aren't great, but they are better than you will have for the next several months, so enjoy. Be down here in the lobby at sunrise to start packing the ships for departure. Tomorrow night you will sleep on the boat, and we will push off first thing the following morning. You both will be working under the direct supervision of Eduardo Santo on the San Pedro."

The two thanked the attendant and headed up to drop their luggage off and clean up before supper. "Not bad," said Ferdinand, "looks clean, and I suppose that is all that we need. That and cotton for my ears to drown out your ridiculous snoring." He added teasingly.

"I don't snore."

"Ha, ha," replied Ferdinand. Hopefully, Rosalie will only discover how much you snore after you are married, and it's too late."

Diego responded by tossing a pillow at him before going in

to clean up for dinner.

CHAPTER TWENTY-FIVE

"Our chief want in life is somebody who will make us do what we can."

RALPH WALDO EMERSON

As Diego and Ferdinand tentatively entered the dining hall, they were struck by the noise and chaos that greeted them. Boisterous voices struggled to be heard, and what sounded like good-natured banter was exchanged between friends and coworkers that seemingly had not seen each other for a while.

As they searched for two empty seats, they spied a very pleasant-looking old man with a long gray beard waving them over. As they approached the table, he addressed them in a very gravelly voice, "Would you happen to be Ferdinand Flores and Diego Ramirez?"

"Yes, I am Deigo, and this is Ferdinand," said Diego reaching out his hand.

Before taking Diego's hand, the man wiped his on a napkin. "I am Eduardo Santo, and you two will be my helpers. I am very pleased to meet you." While the man had a very rugged appearance, something warm and friendly sparkled from his eyes.

"Pleased to meet you too, Mr. Santo, or is it Captain Santo?" asked Ferdinand, extending his hand.

The man let out a very genuine and booming laugh. "No one ever calls me Mr, and I am by no means a captain. I am the ship's cook and caretaker of all live cargo, When I first became the cook, everyone called me 'Cook Eduardo, but it didn't take long for it to be shortened to CookE, which is what I prefer anyway."

CookE motioned for the boys to have a seat. As they waited for the boys' food, they began the process of getting to know each other. CookE started by asking the two about their previous sailing experiences. "We have none," answered Ferdinand timidly, "I hope that isn't a problem. The advertisement and the recruiter said that no experience was necessary."

CookE shook his head, "No problem at all. The crew that will be on top will be well experienced and able to take care of the sailing. You will be working down below with me, preparing and serving meals and taking care of the horses. All you will need is the ability to work hard and listen to what I ask you to do."

"That will be no problem at all," responded Diego. "Ferdinand and I have worked very hard. Me at my father's shop and he at his father's restaurant. We will be happy to do whatever is asked of us."

"Then we will get along just fine," said CookE with a grin. "What brings you on this fine adventure in the first place?" he asked.

When the boys told him their story of Rosalie and Isabelle and their mutual desire for Rosalie and Diego to be able to start their lives together, CookE seemed pleased. "So many young people set out with grandiose dreams of adventure, glory, and riches," he said. "I am glad that your goals are so much nobler."

"Why do you do it?" asked Diego.

"Me? Well, I've been sailing since I was your age, maybe even a little younger. I actually sailed with Christopher Columbus on his very first voyage in 1492." CookE half said, and half yawned. "But that and many other stories can wait for another time. I have a million stories to tell, and I hope I don't bore you, but now it is time for this old man to get some sleep. He stood and tipped his cap. "See you two in the morning. Good night."

"Good night," Diego and Ferdinand responded together. Somehow they didn't think that they would be bored at all by CookE's stories.

CHAPTER TWENTY-SIX

"Do something. Get moving. Be confident. Risk new things. Stick with it. Get on your knees. Then be ready for big surprises."

SAINT ANGELA MERICI

Early the next morning, Diego and Ferdinand heard a loud banging on the door followed by the announcement, "Thirty minutes to be in the lobby." In their case, the wake-up call was unnecessary. Both boys were already awake and staring at the ceiling, awaiting the time for them to go downstairs. The last thing that they wanted to happen was to be late for the first day.

The two quickly dressed, gathered their belongings, and headed for the lobby. When they arrived, several others were already mulling around the room. Attached to the walls were the names of six ships that would make up the fleet which would shortly begin preparations for the New World's journey. Diego and Ferdinand spied the "San Pedro" sign and headed towards it. They found CookE talking to several men in their mid-twenties. When he saw the two boys, he called them over and made the introductions. Both of the men were among the sailing crew and were native to Palos. CookE explained that over half of the sailors were from there and that Palos was known for producing the finest sailors in the world, including the ones who directed Christopher Columbus to the New World.

"If it weren't for Palos sailors and specifically Martin Pinzon and his brother Vincente, Columbus trip would have been over before it started. After Columbus finally got the King and Queen to agree to his voyage, he still had to recruit about ninety men to join his crew. To help him recruit, the King offered a full pardon to any prisoner who was willing to join the mission, but only a few responded." explained CookE.

"Yes," one of the crewmen standing next to CookE chimed in. "The so-called Admiral." he said with disdain, "Didn't have many friends in this town."

"Still doesn't," added the other man.

Diego and Ferdinand were intrigued. "Why is that?" asked Ferdinand.

CookE explained, "Some of the reasons were not entirely his fault. The town resented him because the King and Queen demanded that the town make two caravels available to him for a supposed debt that the town didn't feel it owed. The second reason is that as you know, he was a foreigner, not only was he not from the town or region, he was not even from Spain. Finally, Columbus acted as if he were the most accomplished sailor in the world when everyone knew that the Pinzon's could outsail the man any day."

"So because of all this, people didn't trust him and didn't want to sail with him? That makes sense, but what changed their minds?" questioned Diego.

"The Pinzon brothers did," answered CookE. Martin agreed to captain the Pinta, and Vincentes agreed to do the same for the Nina, leaving Columbus to command the fleet from the out-dated and cumbersome Santa Maria. Once the Pinzon's were aboard, others quickly joined. The Pinzon's gave the journey credibility and gave sailors faith that it could succeed. That is why, you celebrate Columbus in October, but people in this area celebrate Pinzon Day in April. While Columbus grabbed all of the glory and most of the money for himself, most people around here believe that the credit belongs to the Pinzons."

A tall man climbed a makeshift stage that had been erected in the center of the room. As he did so, everyone became quiet. Five other men joined him and formed a semi-circle around him. He introduced himself as Captain Cruz, the San Josef ship captain and the expedition's lead captain. He then introduced the other five captains who stood behind him, each of whom would command their ship. The last captain introduced was Captain Sanchez, the San Pedro captain, on which Diego and Ferdinand were assigned. As he was announced, CookE leaned forward and whispered to the boys, "We are lucky. I've sailed under Sanchez many times. He is a very fair man and an extremely accomplished sailor. Everyone respects him."

After the introductions, the local priest blessed the crew and led them to the docks where he blessed the ships. The sight of the vessels and the vastness of the ocean struck the boys with awe. "Can you believe that we are doing this?" asked Diego.

"It's unreal, seems like a dream -- a little scary too, but there is no turning back now, even if we wanted," replied Ferdinand.

"I can't believe we have never been on a ship before, and now, on our first trip, we are going to be sailing across the ocean. It is wonderful to have one last great adventure with you before settling down with Rosalie," said Diego.

"I have seen pictures of these new galleons, but they are even more impressive in person. It will be interesting to see how they operate," said Ferdinand. "I understand that they are not quite as fast as the caravels or can't carry as much cargo as the old carrack, but they are still pretty fast and can carry a large load."

"I am not sure we will be above board very much of the time to see it in action, but I am sure CookE will be able to teach us the ins and outs of sailing the ship," said Diego.

"I concur; working with CookE will be very enlightening,"

agreed Ferdinand.

The first order of business of the day was to load more than enough food and water for the trip on each of the ships, just to be sure. Then they loaded horses, hay, and a variety of other supplies in three of the ships, but not the other three, which struck Diego and Ferdinand as odd.

"We will have to ask CookE about it later tonight," said Ferdinand.

Late in the afternoon,CookE summoned the boys off the docks to the lower deck to help him begin the evening meal. As they entered the kitchen area, they passed shelves full of dried and salted anchovies and cod, pickled and salted beef and pork, dried grains like chickpeas, lentils and beans, and, of course, hardtack biscuits.

As if reading their minds, CookE said, "For food to remain good at sea, it must be dried. The salt and pickling also help it last. We will try to spice it up and make it as tasty as we can, but there is only so much we can do. You do get used to it after a while, or at least you learn to stomach it."

After preparing, serving, and cleaning up dinner, CookE, Ferdinand and Diego sat down to eat their meals before tending to the horses. Cooke, who was eating his food as if he had not eaten in weeks, looked over to the boys, who were just moving it around on their plates, and laughed. "It will become easier, trust me," he said. "In the meantime, try to eat as much as you can. You will need your strength."

"Hey Cookie," asked Diego, picking up a biscuit, "Why are three of the ships jammed with supplies and horses while three of them only carried supplies for the trip?'

Cookie cleared his throat and looked downcast. "The other three will be full too before they head across the ocean. All six of us will head south to Africa. Then we will dock in Sierre Leone on the west coast and fill their hulls with slaves before we head out. Because I am in charge of all live cargo, I will have to get off the ship and inventory the enslaved people as they are loaded aboard, but you two should stay on the ship. It won't take long."

Diego and Ferdinand were quiet for a moment. "I never thought about the possibility of being on a ship that carried slaves," said Ferdinand. "I don't think I would have liked that at all."

"Me neither," added Diego, "I guess we were lucky that we were not assigned to one."

"It wasn't luck," responded CookE. "I refuse to sail on a ship that carries slaves, and I specifically requested to have you two assigned to me."

Diego and Ferdinand looked at each other surprised. "Why?" asked Ferdinand, "I mean, we are grateful and like working for you, but why did you request us? "

"Yes," Diego chimed in, "Why did you request us, and why do you refuse to work on a ship carrying slaves. Did you work on one before?"

"I guess I do owe you an explanation, and I will answer your questions, but first, let's finish our chores for the day. We have a lot of hungry horses that need to be fed," said CookE. "We'll talk tonight."

CHAPTER TWENTY-SEVEN

"The seven social sins are:

Wealth without work,
Pleasure without conscience,
Knowledge without character,
Commerce without morality,
Science without humanity,
Worship without sacrifice,
Politics without principle.

FREDERICK LEWIS DONALDSON

It took several hours of hard work to feed all of the horses and bed them down for the night. After they finished, CookE, Diego, and Ferdinand cleaned up and headed to the top deck to finally get some air. They found a spot on the ship's bow and sat looking out to the sea ahead and enjoying the stars in the sky.

'I have been sailing since I was younger than you two," began CookE, "But it never grows old," CookE waved his arms toward the sea. "I just can't get enough of the smells, the sounds, or the feel of the sea. I know it sounds cliche, but in a way, I am married to the sea. God knows, no woman would ever have me," he added laughing.

Ferdinand and Diego joined in the laughter but said nothing, giving their mentor a chance to explain why he had chosen them and why he refused to be on a ship with slaves. After a few minutes of awkward silence, CookE began, "As I said, I owe you two an explanation. It was not by chance that you were assigned to me. You see," he said, nodding toward Ferdinand, "when you walked into the recruiting office in Zaragoza, I was there, although I am sure that you did not notice me. I was at a desk behind the recruiter's, looking over some maps. James is a friend of mine, and I was up visiting him when you walked in. James had been on me to join him for the Pillar du Festival for years. Well, anyway, that's not important. What is important is that I was there when you walked through the door."

"I do remember someone sitting at the desk," said Ferdinand, "but I didn't pay that much attention."

"Nor would I have expected that you would," continued CookE, "But I noticed you. You reminded me of me at your age. A young man but still not fully immersed in all the ways of the world. I know that I had no right to -- I mean, I am not your father or anything -- but I wanted to protect you. I thought that if you were assigned to me, I could prevent you from having the same nightmares that have haunted me throughout my life. At least you would not have to travel on the same ship as slaves. Not that I think that I could shield you from the practice of slavery. I don't think that I would want to even if I could. I think everyone should know what is going on and, too many people already like to pretend that it is not or that it is okay. However, knowing about the atrocities and witnessing the horror of them firsthand are two different things indeed. If you ever actually go out on an exploration, you will see enough terrible things. Again, I am sorry, but I specifically asked that you be assigned to me, and after I heard you also signed up, Diego, I asked that you join us. After I met you and heard of the noble reason for you signing up, I thought that maybe I made the right decision."

At first, neither Diego nor Ferdinand knew what to say. It was Ferdinand that broke the silence. "I, for one, cannot possibly thank you enough," he said. I signed on as a quick way to help Diego earn money to start his family and hopefully help others along the way. I certainly, don't want anything to do with slave trade. I am so grateful."

"As am I," echoed Diego. "The thought of also transporting slaves never even occurred to me. I feel guilty just making money off this enterprise now."

"Look, boys," said CookE, "You had no idea that joining up to deliver "supplies" to the settlers and explorers of the new world would include slaves. Traders consider slaves to be commodities, just like all other merchandise, so they would not make any distinction. I am not surprised that they failed to mention that to you when you signed up. How could you know? Me, I know, but what can I do. I hate slavery with everything that I am, but I have been a sailor all of my life. Right or wrong, it is all I know. So I stay below board and refuse to ride on a boat that carries human cargo. Perhaps that is not enough, but I don't know what else I can do?"

Diego and Ferdinand were quiet for a while. "So riding on a ship carrying slaves was as bad as I would imagine it would be?" asked Diego.

CookE remarked, "I am sure that it is even much worse than you or anyone who has not experienced it could ever imagine." The boys could see that CookE was becoming very emotional and was starting to cry.

"You don't have to tell us if it is too difficult," said Ferdinand.

"No, said CookE, "It is important that you know. Everyone must know. I tell everybody that I meet what it is like. I admit it might be like spitting on a raging fire, but I hope that if I can turn just a few people against slavery, and they convert a few others and, well, you know. I don't expect an end to slavery any time soon, but I have to at least speak out against it, even if only to a tiny audience. I just didn't want you to have to experience it the way I did. I may never recover, and in some ways, I hope that I never do. I mean, as devastated as I am by what I have witnessed, I can hardly bear to think about what it is like for the men, women, and children, who have not only witnessed but experienced the horrors. Maybe by remembering them and empathizing with them, I will always be driven to tell their stories and to hold them in my prayers."

"Your's sounds like a very worthy mission," said Ferdinand, "But along with telling their stories, why don't you also write their stories? That way, you can have them printed and pass them out everywhere you go so more people will see them."

"Great idea," replied CookE, "but alas, while I can read, write, do math and tell a good story, I am not as good as writing one.."

"That's okay, " replied Ferdinand, "You can tell us the stories, and we will write them down for you."

CookE was touched. "You would do that for me? That would be wonderful! That way, more people would get the message, and the message could continue to circulate even after I have stopped," he laughed.

"We would love to," replied Diego. "It would just be our very small way of joining in your mission. Plus, after what you have saved us from experiencing, it is the least we can do."

"Sounds great, boys! Thank you," said CookE, "But do you mind if we start tomorrow? This old man needs to get some sleep."

CHAPTER TWENTY-EIGHT

"You may choose to look the other way, but you can never say again that you did not know."

WILLIAM WILBERFORCE

Each day of the following week was identical to the one before. CookE, Diego, and Ferdinand would wake up before the sun and begin breakfast preparations for their crew of thirty. After breakfast was served and cleared, the team would grab a quick bite before tending to the horses.

The first chore was feeding hay and a combination of oats and barley. Miguel, would then come down and join them. Miguel, a young man around the same age as Diego and Ferdinand, was the ship's cooper. When CookE first introduced Miguel to the boys, he explained, "Miguel might have the most important job of anyone on the ship. He is the cooper, and as such, it is his job to see that those barrels are well maintained," CookE explained, motioning to the enormous wooden kegs in the back of the hull.

The first thing that Miguel did was to inspect each barrel to be sure that everything was tight and that there were no leaks. "If we aren't careful and we lose too much water, we could be in grave danger of dying from dehydration," he explained. "It is ironic to think about the real possibility of dying from a lack of water on a ship in the middle of the ocean, but as you know our bodies cannot process sea water."

He would then carefully open one of the kegs and begin to carefully fill buckets. Diego and Ferdinand would then carry buckets up to the main deck, careful not to spill any, while CookE carried buckets to the horses. Then, Miguel would carefully measure the amount of water used and record it in a journal before replacing the lid tightly and making whatever adjustments had to be made to the barrels.

After feeding and watering the animals, CookE, Diego, and Ferdinand would alternate walking the horses around the open spaces of the hull, while the other two cleaned out the stalls. All three of them grew fond of the horses as they got to know each animal's individual personality.

The three would usually have an hour or two in the afternoon which they spent napping from their early rising and hard work before they repeated the process around dinner time. In the evenings the three would climb to the top deck and sit at the same spot as the first night and CookE would tell his stories. It usually fell on Ferdinand to write down the accounts as he was certainly the more accomplished writer, but Diego also took a turn sometimes in order to give his friend a break

They had all agreed that CookE would begin by recounting how it came to be that he found himself a cook and caretaker of slaves in the first place. "I didn't start out to be a cook," he began. I was a sailor for fourteen years and a fine good one, before I switched from working on the deck under the direct command of Captain Pinzon to becoming the ship's cook."

"I was twenty-seven years old, when Christopher Columbus came to town after having received the backing he needed from King Ferdinand and Queen Isabella. Like most all of the sailors in town I was approached about joining Columbus' crew. And like most of the sailors in town I was very reluctant for the reasons I have already explained."

"You didn't trust Columbus and you felt that your town being required to provide two caravels at their own expense was unfair," confirmed Ferdinand.

"Precisely," said CookE. "It was widely believed that any man from Palo who signed up was betraying his own town, and besides we weren't sure of the plan that was presented to us. Several men had sailed with the Portugeese captains down along the coast of Africa, and many believed that would actually be the shortest route to the Indies. Columbus' plan was new and untested, and while many of us were intrigued, we also had our doubts."

"But as the story goes," he continued. "Martin Pinzon was eventually drawn in by his strong sense of adventure, and with Martin on board many other sailors, including me, joined as well. I sailed on the Nina. It was my first time sailing under Vincentes Pinzon and on a ship as fine as the Nina. I was thrilled. The Pinta and the Nina were both marvels to behold, They were smaller, faster, and more agile than any ship I had ever seen. I was glad to have joined early and been able to get assigned to the Nina, although being assigned to the Pinta under Martin might have been even better. Those who signed up last got the misfortune of sailing on the Santa Maria."

"But why make the Santa Maria, the flagship?" asked Diego.

"Simply because of its size," answered CookE. It was by far the largest of the three boats, but it was slow and hard to maneuver. Even Columbus hated that ship, but as I say it was the biggest so he made it the flagship under the direct command of Juan de la Cosa, who was well seasoned and much respected. Unfortunately, because the admiral himself also sailed on the ship, de la Cosa was often overshadowed, even though the day to day commands were supposed to come from him. He and Columbus never got along, and were often at odds with each other. It almost led to a mutiny a couple of times.

I will never forget the feeling of excitement we all had as we prepared for the trip. The thrill of a new adventure was intoxicating, and once we had committed to the voyage, we were full of anticipation. We could not help but feel that we were about to be involved in something that would be monumental, although we had no idea what that would turn out to be."

"Three were ninety of us in all and because many of us had sailed on different ships under different captains, we gathered to go over the whistles to make sure that we all knew what each whistle meant,": said CookE.

"I have been hearing whistles," said Ferdinand, "Mostly when we were helping Miguel carry water up to the deck. Don't hear them so much down below, but I was meaning to ask you what they all meant. Actually, all of this is so new to us and we are filled with so many questions it is hard to figure out which questions to ask when."

CookE laughed,"You see, sometimes voices get muffled by the sounds of the wind and waves, but a whistle seems to have a way of cutting through it all. That is why over the years sailors have developed a system of whistles to transmit orders. As we sail, I will teach you what each one means. While the codes used are pretty much universal, some captains use a slight variation, which is why you better be sure everyone understands the meaning of the whistles before you set sail. Captain Sanchz of this ship uses pretty much the standard version."

"Finally, on 3 August 1492, the famous journey began. The three ships headed south toward the Canary Islands," Continued CookE before he was interrupted by Diego.

"That is just what we are doing as well, but why sail south if the idea was to reach Asia by sailing west?" he asked.

"Good question," remarkedCookE, who always encouraged the boys to ask questions. "We do it so that we can pick up slaves and catch the trade winds which will help us tremendously.. Columbus and crew did it for the trade winds as well as to make final preparations for the voyage. They also wanted to recruit some sailors from the Canary Islands who are also considered extremely talented. A final reason was that Columbus was out to reach the riches of Asia, and it was calculated that the

Canary Islands and the desired part of Asia were situated on the same latitude. Therefore, by sailing south first, Columbus could take the guesswork out of navigating the ships. He merely would have to sail due west from the islands, which with the use of a compass, astrolabe, and quadrant was very doable. No need to try to figure out the correct angle to sail."

"That makes good sense," said Ferdinand.

"Yes, not only did it make good sense, but the plan turned out to be particularly fortuitous for us, because after only a few days at sea, Santa Maria already had a problem. It's rudder was beginning to pull away from the ship itself. It was Martin Pinzon who came up with a temporary fix that would allow us to make it to the Canary Islands where it could be permanently fixed. It would never have made it across the ocean without being repaired I am pretty sure that it was 9 August 1492 when we pulled into the port of La Gomera.."

"It is rumored that Christopher Columbus was romantically involved with Beatriz de Bobalilla, the beautiful widow and governess of La Gomera, the port city of the Canary Islands. She was known to be one of Columbus' main supporters, and was actually responsible for giving the sugar cane cuttings that were later transplanted in the New World. Whether they were actually involved with each other, I don't know. I never put much stock in rumors, and besides, it was never any of my business," explained CookE.

"So how long was it before you were able to resume your voyage?' questioned Diego.

"It wasn't until 6 September 1492, just a little under a month, before we finally set sail again," said CookE. "We traveled without any sign of land for thirty-five days. The estimation for the crossing was only four weeks. It was obvious to most of us that Columbus had greatly underestimated the distance to the East from traveling west. Of course, back then we didn't know just how badly he had underestimated it, or that there was a continent in the way. As the days wore on, we became more frustrated and worried. As we approached the thirty day mark, a debate arose among the men whether it would be better to turn around and hope that we had enough supplies to make it home or to continue on and possibly perish at sea."

"Columbus for his part would not hear of turning back. I don't know if you would call him brave, stubborn or foolhardy, but he knew what he desired and was willing to risk much to get it. Just when the crew was on the verge of mutiny," remembered CookE, "we all heard the cry, Eureka! No single word had ever sounded so good in my entire life. Loud and boisterous cries echoed throughout the ships as the sailors on all three vessels hooted and hollered and waved to each other. It was 12 October 1942, a day that will be remembered forever."

. "As the ships drew closer to the land," recounted Cooke, "We were greeted by the most beautiful sight in the world. The land was absolutely beautiful. There were pristine beaches as far as we could see that were lined with huge palm trees. I was filled with a feeling that I will always remember for as long as I live. It was a combination of relief that we would indeed survive our journey and the knowledge that we were a part of something incredible -- something that, for better or worse, would change the course of history forever."

CHAPTER TWENTY-NINE

"We need a seat at the table ...If we're not at the table, we're probably on the menu."

ROBERTO MUKARP BORRERO

After a few days at sea the Canary Islands and the West Coast of Africa became visible. The ships veered east to pick up their shipment of human cargo. The two friends stood looking over the side of the ship. Looking at his friend, Ferdinand said, "Missing her greatly today?"

"Pretty obvious, huh," replied Diego. "I just never thought that I would ever be so far away from her. I am sorry, the last thing I would ever want to do is to bring you down, especially since I am being separated from Rosalie for several months, while you are separated from Isabelle for." Diego stopped short.

"I get it," replied Ferdinand, "That is why I am so very grateful to you for accompanying me on this voyage, and to Rosalie for being supportive of the idea. You are right, I am very familiar with the feeling of being separated from the woman I love, but you never get used to it. Know that I share your pain, as does Rosalie."

"Can I ask you something?" said Diego.

"You can always ask me anything." replied Ferdinand.

"I know how very much you loved and still love Isabelle, no one would ever question that. But how is it that, as far as I know, you never visit her grave?"

Ferdinand smiled, "Because she is not there. I mean her body might be but she is not. She is with God and with me and you and Rosalie and everyone that she loves. I know that visiting a grave side helps some people connect with loved ones who have died, and I think that is wonderful for them, but it is not necessary for me. I connect with Isabelle everyday of my life, through both the good memories and the pangs of pain which I still experience on a daily basis. I read the final letter she wrote to us every night before I go to sleep. And everytime my mind goes to her, I stop and say a prayer for her and for everyone that she loves. Sometimes as I relax before sleep and occasionally throughout the day, I can feel her with me. Not in a physical or ghostly way, but I feel that our souls are connecting. It is really hard to explain, but it is real. In some ways it is not unlike that night Rosalie, you, and I sat praying for Isabelle outside her garden wall, and the experience we shared. We all felt her presence as she bid us farewell on her way to her afterlife, We never have even discussed the experience with each other because we didn't have to talk about it. Having experienced the connection we didn't need it explained. I think it is safe to say that none of us have talked about it with others either, because explaining it to someone who did not experience it would be futile."

Diego thought for a moment, "I guess in some ways that it is also like how your father knew something was wrong with your grandfather without being told, and you knew something was wrong with Isabelle as well," he said.

"Absolutely," replied Ferdinand, "When the love between two people is strong enough there is a connection that ties them together, a bond that can never be broken. You and Rosalie also have that bond, my friend."

"Thank you," said Diego. "Talking with you always has lifted my spirits. So if I am thinking about Rosalie some night and I turn my thoughts to God in prayer for her, do you think that at some point I will feel her soul with mine?'

"I don't think so, I know it," assured Ferdinand. Oh sometimes you may feel the connection between the two of you, and other times you may not; but have faith, the connection is there."

The two boys continued to watch the African continent grow closer before turning around and heading down to begin their afternoon chores.

After all the chores, Diego, Ferdinand and CookE returned to their customary spot on the deck, so that CookE could once again continue to share his saga with the boys. "Exploring the islands on that first trip with Columbus was quite the adventure. On our very first day of exploration, we encountered the Taino, the inhabitants of the islands. They were such good natured, gentle people who posed no threat to us. They willingly shared with us their yams, corn, beans, peanuts, peppers, and tobacco. For protein, the Taino hunted small animals that included lizards and birds; they also ate seafood. All of which they very willingly shared. They were good looking people that Columbus called the color of canary, meaning the same as the people on the Canary Islands —definitely darker than you or I, but not as dark as the people from mainland Africa."

"They also showed us how they grew their crops by a system of shifting agriculture whereby the forests are burned and the ashes raked into mounds and the crops are then planted in the mounds. We had never seen anything like this before, it was fascinating,"

Both Diego and Ferdinand were intrigued. "What were their homes like?"asked Ferdinand.

"Their houses were made of logs with thatched roofs," CookE answered. Their settlements ranged from just a few houses to a group of up to three-thousand families. On the trees outside their homes they hung these things that they called hammocks, they were made from netting type material and were wonderful for taking naps, great contraptions, several of us took one back with us to use in Spain."

"So, there was no hostility between the explorers and the Taino at all?' asked Ferdinand.

"Not with us, not at the beginning anyway. They did live in constant fear of the tribe they called the Caribs who lived on different Islands against who they had to defend themselves. Columbus actually offered to protect the Taino from the Caribs," laughed CookE. "How ironic? If only they knew that the people who pledged to protect them would be the cause of their demise, but that didn't happen on the first stop that we made."

"On that very first day", continued CookE, "We all greeted the Taino's with whatever trinkets that we could find. Then to our surprise we saw them rowing out to our boats with handmade jewelry and other gifts for us. They were riding in crafts that they called canoes that were made from carved out logs, some of them were large enough to hold one-hundred men. They apparently had no iron with which to form weapons,because the only thing that they had on the tips of their spears were sharp sea shells, but they were able develop poison and a spray that would temporarily blind their attackers to help defend them from the Caribs. Columbus did claim their land for Spain and announced that he was their new governor, as was his agreement with King Ferdinand and Queen Isabella, but I don't think that the Taino actually understood all that would entail."

"So the first landing was on the Island of the Bahamas?" asked Diego.

"That is correct, " said CookE, "But then we headed off to explore some of the neighboring islands that were mostly also inhabited by the Taino people. We did encounter some of the vicious Caribs that terrorized the Taino people and dispatched with them as was in keeping with the promise to help the Taino as well as to avenge the killing of a couple of our men. With their lack of weaponry, it really wasn't much of a battle."

"It was when we made our last couple of landings," CookE continued, "That everything changed. Columbus knew that we were drawing towards the end of our adventure, and while he considered the journey a tremendous success, he needed tangible items to bring back to Spain. He needed gold, silver, and slaves to justify the king's and queen's investment in his voyage. That is when the looting, raping, kidnapping and murder began, all in the name of Christ and King. I saw and experienced images that, along with the suffering of the African slaves later in my life, will torment me forever. Once it started it was like a raging fire, I don't think that even Columbus could have stopped it, even if he wanted. The Taino men did try to defend themselves as well as their children and their women, but they were ill equipped to do so." CookE began to get extremely emotional.

"That was not what I signed on to do," he stated now crying hard. "I joined the expedition to find a shorter route to Asia, to deal in trading with the Asian people, to serve my God and my country. I did not come to pillage and murder innocent people. To do it in the name of God, only made what we had done more obscene, it justified nothing."

Diego and Ferdinand sat speechless. "I am sorry boys, but that is it for now. It is time for this old man to get some sleep."

CHAPTER THIRTY

"If you judge a book by its cover, you might miss out on an amazing story."

ANONYMOUS

The sea was very rough the next day, and the winds howled. It was difficult to prepare the meals and CookE and the boys had to work extra hard to keep the horses calm. Suddenly, Miguel ran down the steps shouting, "CookE! CookE! CookE! The captain needs you NOW!"

CookE pushed past Diego and Ferdinand on his way up to the deck. The two boys quickly followed in pursuit. When they emerged they were greeted by total chaos as crew men desperately tried to bail water off the deck with anything that they could find. The three could easily see fear in their comrades' eyes, as no matter how hard they tried, more water seemed to be breaching the top of the boat and coming in than they were able to bail out. The situation was evidently perilous, one of the crew inadvertently turned a sail the wrong way and shifted the boat to its side, where it took on a huge amount of water. As soon as the captain saw CookE, he called them over and motioned for Diego and Ferdinand to follow.

"I need your help," said Captain Sanchez pleadingly as he looked CookE straight in the eyes.

As CookE nodded his assent, the captain pulled Ferdinand and Diego close to him so that they could clearly hear. "I need you to go to each man on this ship. Tell them that they are to follow CookE's commands exactly, even if they don't seem to make sense. Let them know that if any of them hesitate, even a second, they will have to answer to me."

Ferdinand and Diego set out to follow the captain's orders as Captain Sanchez handed the whistle to CookE. After the captain's message was relayed, CookE blew a series of signals to which the crew responded by raising or lowering the appropriate sail. The crew frantically raised, lowered, and shifted sails in response to CookE's whistled orders. His final order was three long whistles which caused the crew to drop all of their ropes at once and hit the deck. CookE also pushed the captain, Diego, and Ferdinand to the deck as the boat toppled to its left side leaving the crew battling to stay on board. Right when the ship was on the verge of capsizing its momentum stopped and it started swaying to the right. After a few seconds, the ship was again upright and to the amazement of the crew most of the water that had threatened to sink the boat had spilled out. The little that remained was easily and quickly bailed out.

The ship erupted with cheers and the crew commenced hugging each other and CookE. CookE immediately dropped to his knees and everyone followed his clue, together they gave thanks to Mother Mary and her sweet Son.

When the three were alone again below deck, Diego exclaimed, "That was absolutely amazing!"

Ferdinand agreed, "Yes! It was. How did you know that would work?"

CookE answered, still apparently shaken by their experience, "I didn't know it would work, but I knew it was the only thing that could work. The rest was in the hands of God. He was with us here today, boys."

That night after all of the day's chores were finished, CookE told the boys that he was not only physically, but emotionally exhausted and he was going to turn in for the night. The story of Columbus' first voyage would have to wait until the next night.

After CookE took his leave, Diego said, "I just realized something."

"What's that?" asked Ferdinand.

"Well we know that CookE is able to choose to work on boats that do not carry slaves, and we know that he was able to request and receive us as his assistants. But I don't see other crewmen, especially cooks having that much sway with the captains, even one who have sailed for a long time. So now I figure that it is because he is such an exceptional seaman that he is an asset to have onboard in case of an emergency, like the one that we had today."

Ferdinand thought for a while, "That makes sense he acknowledged, and it was quite amazing today; but there are still a few things that puzzle me about his story that we have heard so far."

"Like what?" asked Diego. He had some questions himself, but wanted to know if they were the same as his friends.

"Well," said Ferdinand, "I understand how he would be so disillusioned by what Columbus and his men did to the Tainos that it would have soured him on exploring, I think I would have had the same reaction. But my question is then, why sail to the New World at all, and especially why ever sail there on a ship that carried slaves in the first place?"

"I have the same questions," replied Diego. "I hope that if we are patient these questions will be answered for us. CookE is a wealth of knowledge, but as much as he wants us to know his stories, I also feel that they are very difficult for him to tell. He is certainly interesting."

CHAPTER THIRTY-ONE

"There are many humorous things in the world, among them, the white man's notion that he is less savage than the other savages."

MARK TWAIN

After the day of the near disaster the following days of the voyage were pretty unremarkable; each day mirroring the one before it. As Ferdindand and Diego worked alongside CookE, they grew to respect the humble and knowledgeable man. He may not have had much education, but he was wise in ways that many more educated men that they knew were not. His manner in dealing with the horses belied a gentle and caring spirit that was rooted in his strong faith. The boys' initial liking of CookE grew into a strong friendship. CookE, for his part, felt the same way about the boys. He was glad that he had requested them. The three enjoyed working together, and they especially enjoyed their time on the deck in the cool evenings, enjoying the stars and learning from CookE's exploits.

After taking the night before off, Ferdinand and Diego were eager for the remainder of CookE's telling of Columbus' first voyage. "Well, as I said last time", he began, "I was sickened after I experienced the harsh treatment of the Tainos. I wanted nothing to do with it, but desertion is not an option for a sailor unless he wants to be thrown overboard. Maritime law requires the death penalty for the crime of mutiny. All that I could do was to go about my duties as a sailor and avoid personally engaging in any of the atrocities. I was thrilled when at last it was time for us to leave for our last stop, before returning to Spain, but I knew that the drive to justify the expedition with riches and the ensuing pillaging would be just as bad. I was helpless to stop it, which made me feel even sicker inside. I just wanted the trip to be over and return to Spain where I planned to settle down and never sail to the Americas again."

"I assume that the final stop was Hispanolia," said Ferdinand, "I remember learning about the exploration in school, that is except for the murdering and pillaging and a few other key parts."

"That is correct," said CookE. "It was the last and shortest lag of the trip, but it was difficult from the beginning. On our way to the island, the Santa Maria came too close to shore and beached itself. The damage was extensive and the decision was made to abandon it. Much of the wood from it was eventually used to build the first Spanish fort, and settlement in the New World. They named it La Navidad, because it was on Christmas that the Santa Maria was beached. It was from there that Columbus and the crew ran their raids on the Tainos. Prior to the landing on Hispaniola, the Pinta which was captained by Martin Pinzon, was separated from us. So Columbus set sail on the Nina to find them. He did so a couple of days later. Columbus actually accused Pinzon of separating on purpose to search for gold himself. After a bitter argument between the two, the ships headed back to Hispaniola to restock for the long journey home. Finally on January 16, 1493, the Nina and Pinta headed off towards Spain."

"If you came with three boats and had to abandon the largest one there," asked Ferdinand, "How did everyone fit?"

"It was difficult," responded CookE, "And it would have

been impossible if Columbus had not left thirty-six men behind to man the fort while he was gone, But you must remember that the Nina and Pinta were caravels, and unlike this galleon, there were no lower decks. This meant that whether you were on duty or not, you were on the same deck as those who were. It is very hard to sleep with the working crew having to step over you to do their jobs. It was a very hard journey. Despite the difficulty, my comrades morale was very high as they considered their journey a tremendous success. I however was totally broken. I could not get the images of the slaughtered men, women, and children out of my mind," bemoaned CookE. "And when we had pulled into a Portuguese port so close to home, I thought the saga was almost over; only to find ourselves detained by some Portuguese who were hostile to us and our journey. By the time our release was obtained and we pulled back into Spain it was mid-March. I was never so glad to be home in my life. I made myself a promise to never again sail across the ocean."

"But you did. How come, if you had promised not to go, and the images still haunt you?" Asked Diego.

"That my young friends is a story for tomorrow. Good night," said CookE as he rose to go to bed for the evening.

CHAPTER THIRTY-TWO

"The best way to teach people is by telling a story."

KENNETH BLANCHARD

The following evening Diego and Ferdinand settled in their usual spot anxious to hear the next part of CookE's story. All day it was all either of them could think about. When they had a chance to speak with each other, they spent the time theorizing what could have made CookE return on a ship, especially a slave ship, after his horrifying experience.

As the three friends settled in, CookE resumed, " Like I said last night. I was totally crushed by what I had witnessed, and even though I did not personally take part in the pillaging, raping, and murder, I couldn't shake the feeling that I nevertheless had blood on my hands."

"But what could you have done?"asked Ferdinand with empathy for his new friend. "You couldn't stop it, and you could not have known that it would happen."

"That is what I kept telling myself over and over," replied CookE meloncholily, "but even if I could get my mind to believe it, my heart would not. So I tried to put the past behind me. I kept busy working the docks and sometimes making deliveries up and down the coast of Europe. I kept off the ships headed to

America, but I did keep in touch with many of my mates who made several expeditions there. Several sailed with Columbus on his second, third and fourth trip to the New World. Others traveled with Hernando Cortes, but all told stories pretty similar to mine; they all included the same atrocities to innocent ill-equipped people. I wanted no part in it."

"What changed?"asked Diego, unable to restrain his curiosity.

"Well," said CookE, "I guess you could say that I changed.

CHAPTER THIRTY-THREE

CookE's Story

"If Slavery is not wrong, then nothing is."

ABRAHAM LINCOLN

"Do you remember when I said that the recruiter who signed you up for the trip was a friend of mine?"

Ferdinand and Diego both nodded.

"His name is James, and he and I have been friends for years, back when I was still Eduardo, long before I became CookE. James has a rather lovely sister named Maria," continued CookE. Maria is a nurse, and a very fine one at that, Maria and her family live in the port city of Sierra Leone where Maria is the head of nursing at the local hospital. James talked me into going with him to visit Maria and her family over Christmas 1518. That visit changed my life forever, and in a way, I believe redeemed my soul."

"Wow!"replied Diego, "We can hardly wait to hear."

"1518 that was the same year that King Charles authorized Spain to ship enslaved people directly from Africa to the Americas, wasn't it?" asked Ferdinand.

"Yes, and that dramatically increased the slave trade to the New World." replied CookE. "Originally the Spanish settlers tried to enslave the native people, but that failed for several reasons. A main reason was that the natives often succommed to diseases from the Spaniards and died. Secondly, the natives knew the land much better than their captors and had many ties to unenslaved friends and families; this led to many escapes and uprisings. Finally, the king and queen wanted the conquests to yield subjects for them to rule, and enslaved people were not considered subjects. So enslaving the natives became taboo, especially the ones who agreed to convert to Christianity."

"As times passed and the conquistadors sailed, it became apparent that, although there were some heavy concentrations of gold and precious metals in some areas, the real wealth was to be gained from agriculture and natural resources above ground. And suddenly African slaves came into high demand. Unfortunately for settlers, until August of that year any slave shipped to the New World had to first be shipped to Europe. When the edict was signed and charters granted to the King's friends, all that abruptly changed, and Sierra Leone became a major slave shipping port."

"Maria, and her family are remarkable people. From the time James introduced me to them, I felt completely at home, I felt like family. After I settled into the extra bedroom, James knocked on the door, and let me know that dinner was ready. As I entered the dining room Julius, Maria's husband, was putting the food on the table.

"Smells great, my dear," said Maria, smiling at her husband. "Because I work so many crazy hours," said Maria looking at me, "Julius cooks most of the meals. Actually he has become a much better cook than I ever could be."

Julius smiled in response. The family took their normal seats with Maria and Julius on the ends, the children Abeni — a sweet five-year old girl on one side, and Abdoul —her older brother of fifteen— on the other. James and I were each assigned seats across from each other. Finally, Julius led the group in prayer.

Dinner was fantastic. The food tasted great, and everyone engaged in lively conversation and much good-natured teasing. It was easy to tell that, while James enjoyed teasing his little sister, Maria was well able to handle it and give it back as well. Their love for each other was evident.

After dinner and dessert, Maria excused herself and announced that she would be back in a couple of hours. Abeni and Abdoul were assigned to clearing the table and doing dishes, as Julius invited James and me to relax in the parlor. "Did Maria have to go back to work at the hospital?"I asked as we settled in the chairs.

"Not exactly," replied Julius.

"My sister spends her evening tending to the injured and sick enslaved men, women, and children who are caged down by the docks," explained James.

"Is that part of her duty as a nurse at the hospital?"I asked.

"No." replied Julius, "That is part of her duty as a Christian. My wife is a wonderful woman who sees God in everyone. To the slave traders, those people may be nothing more than chattel, but Maria recognizes them as children of God. She can't stop the slave trade, and she has no control over what happens to them when they are marched onto the ships. While she can, she does everything in her power to ease their pain and suffering while they are still here. That is just who she is."

"So the guards don't mind her helping the slaves?"

"Not at all; they see it as protecting their product. Anything that keeps the slaves alive adds to their bottom line," explained James.

"It is amazing how badly some people can treat other human beings," lamented Julius. "But James tells me that you have sailed with Columbus and have seen first hand the horrors inflicted upon innocents. I understand it was quite upsetting to you."

"I may never get over it," I replied, mournfully remembering the past.

CHAPTER THIRTY-FOUR

CookE's Story Part Two

"Whatsoever you do to the least of these brothers, that you do unto me."

JESUS CHRIST, MATTHEW 25:40

"After dinner the following night, when Maria announced that she would again be back in a few hours, I spoke up, 'Would it be okay if I go with you?"I asked.

Maria hesitated, " I am not sure, Eduardo. Where I am going, you will see many inhumane things. James has told us that you are still suffering from your previous experiences. Do you want to relive them?"

"No, I don't ever want to relive them, but I do, every day and night. I just can't get the images out of my mind. That is why I want to come with you. I want to help. The last time I was faced with atrocities happening around me, I was helpless to do anything. I hope that now, faced with similar cruelty, I might be able to help in some way, even if only in a tiny one."

Maria looked over to James who merely nodded, "I too

would like to go along and help if possible," he said. Maria nodded, and the three of us headed out the door.

As we walked, we talked about what we were to encounter and what would be asked of each of us. "I just want to prepare you the best I can for what you will experience, although no words can adequately do so. If you know in advance what to expect, it might help," said Maria. "The encampment is split into two different yards. In the larger yard, the men and boys are kept; the other is home to the women and girls."

"The loud cries from the men, women, and children who have been mercilessly ripped away from their homes and families will assault your senses before you arrive at the camp. Their cries can be heard at all hours of the day and night," continued Maria. "Even grown men who were once proud tribal leaders and strong warriors can be heard screaming and crying as they try to comprehend the unimaginable."

"James, when we get there," Maria said to her brother, "I need you to get some clean water for the men. When I was there last night, the supply was running low. The buckets are too heavy for me to carry. I asked the guards to fill them as they are supposed to as part of their jobs, but if I know them, they probably did not."

James nodded his assent.

"Eduardo," she continued, "I need you to come with me to the women's side. I have to check on Eunie who is about to give birth to her first child. Before I do that, I want to introduce you to Fugra and her daughter, Tianna. Tianna is only eight years old but is extremely bright. I have been trying to teach Tianna Spanish, but I have so much to do that I hardly have time, and she must learn."

"Of course," I said, "I am willing to do whatever it takes to help, but if you don't mind, why is it so important to teach Tianna Spanish?" I was beginning to think that Maria was only trying to find something for me to do, that would be easy so that I might be spared some painful memories.

"For two reasons," replied Maria. "First, if a slave can speak Spanish, there is a decent chance that they will be purchased by someone who is looking for a slave to work inside their home, especially if it is a girl. If Tianna is chosen, she would be spared the rough, backbreaking job of working the fields. Being a slave is a travesty that should not happen to anyone, but there are different levels of horrible, and working conditions for a house slave are much better than those of a field slave. Secondly, if we can teach Tianna enough Spanish while we are with her, I hope that she will pass some on to Fugra, and perhaps they will both be sold together and not split up. Fugra's husband — Tianna's father —Teagu, was killed trying to protect them from the slavers. I don't know if we can, but if we could at least keep them together, perhaps they can help each other through the nightmare that awaits them. If we can't, the horror of being separated will only add to their misery.` `

"Thank you for allowing me to try to teach her," I said. "I will do my very best."

As we approached the compound, the sounds of the cries and moans grew louder. Even with Maria's preparing us for the sounds, we shuddered and were filled with deep sadness. Guards were stationed outside the fence at fifty-foot intervals. "Not much chance of escape, that is for sure," remarked James. "I suppose that if they tried, they would get shot for their efforts?"

"No," Maria responded, "If getting shot was the result of an escape attempt, many, many of them would go for it. No, they don't shoot them if they can help it. Instead, they bring the men back to be examples to the others of what happens if you try to escape. They are savagely beaten and whipped in front of the others. If it is a repeat offender, they may even have a hand or a foot cut off. It is horrific, to say the least."

Because the guard at the gate was well acquainted with Maria, we were allowed in as soon as she introduced James and me. From the moment that I met Fugra and Tianna, I knew two things. I could tell that they were deeply heartbroken and that they were also extremely kind and intelligent underneath their sadness.

Fugra led Tianna and me off to a corner of the compound that was the quietest spot that could be found. Then she spoke something to me in a language that I had never heard before and then looked at Tianna. “Thank you,” Tianna translated, apparently from the Spanish which Maria had been able to teach her. Then Fugra headed off to help Maria tend to the sick and injured.

Tianna and I sat on the ground, She was an eager student, and as Maria said, was extremely bright. I began by teaching her words and phrases using any props around to help. She soaked everything in. My time with Tianna flew by quickly, when Maria and James came to get me, it was hard to believe that two hours had passed.

As I stood to leave, Tianna looked at me with her big brown eyes, “Thank you,” she said slowly, “Good-bye.”

“Tomorrow?” I asked, “Can I come tomorrow?”

For the first time that evening, Tianna smiled and nodded. My heart melted and I became determined to teach her as much Spanish as possible in the little time we had.

The next day after Maria and Julius went to work, and their kids were finishing their last week at school, I went shopping with James. I had to find some props that would help me teach Tianna that evening. We bought common everyday items, like a ball, dish, knife, fork, spoon, towel, and a large case for carrying the items. Earlier that morning, as l I watched Maria and her family share breakfast, all that I could think was, “What if it happened to them?” If you lived in the wrong part of Africa, it could happen to you. I became more determined than ever that if I could do anything to stop Fruga and Tianna from being separated, there was nothing that I wouldn't do.

That night's lesson with Tianna was even more productive than the night before. This young girl's aptitude for learning was truly amazing. When Fruga came by a couple of times to check on us, she proudly demonstrated that which I had taught Tianna the night before. Not only was Tianna a great student, apparently she was also a great teacher.

On the way home I ran an idea I had by Maria to see what she thought. "What if I came here by myself in the morning from about 9 o'clock to 11 and again in the afternoon from 1 o'clock to 3."

"You mean as well as the evening session?"Maria asked.

"Yes," I responded, "If it is not too much. What do you think?"

"I think it would be wonderful, but not much of a restful Christmas break for you."she responded.

"Believe me," I said, "Helping Tianna and Fruga has done more for my spirit and my health than all the rest in the world could do. I am so grateful for the opportunity."

"Okay, then," Maria said with a smile, "I will talk with the head of the camp, but I don't see it as a problem."

Tianna was thrilled to hear about her increased lessons. She could not get enough learning. She was attentive throughout the lessons, and finally we reached the point where we could have some simple conversations. Once we reached that point, her Spanish fluency just exploded, and while not as capable of a Spanish speaker as her daughter, Fruga also improved greatly.

That Christmas Maria and James had decided that they would stay home and spend the day with their family. I agreed that it was a good idea, but I wanted to at least see Tianna that morning, so I broke away for just a short time, to say Merry Christmas and give her a small doll I had bought her as a Christmas present. After a short visit, I stood to leave. As I did so, Tianna ran into my arms crying. "I am sorry that I couldn't get you anything for Christmas," she said in tears.

"You have given me more than you will ever know," I said, "Your friendship means so much to me." With that she gave me a smile that reached from ear to ear — a Christmas present that I will cherish forever. To this day, the image of her smile is what I concentrate on when I am haunted by images of the past, and I find my peace.

CHAPTER THIRTY-FIVE

CookE's Story Part Three

"I think slavery is the next thing to hell. If a person would send another into bondage, he would, it appears to me, be bad enough to send him into hell if he could."

HARRIET TUBMAN

Christmas Day was magnificent. I felt spiritually and mentally healthier than I had in twenty-five years. Julius outdid himself in the kitchen, and everyone enjoyed exchanging presents and singing Christmas songs. After the meal the kids were once again assigned kitchen and dishes duty, while the adults retired to the parlor. It was then that James shared the news with his sister that he had been dreading to share all day, because he didn't want to dampen the family's Christmas. "He just won't do it, Sis," he said, "I tried and I tried, but he just won't budge."

I could see the disappointment and panic in Maria's eyes. "What are we going to do? "She asked. The boat sails in seven days."

"Excuse me," I interrupted. "Who won't do what? Just what is the issue here?"

James hesitated just a second before he answered, "I

was able to assign a man to the ship on which the slaves are to be transported. He would not be able to lessen the misery that the slaves will experience, but he did agree to work with Tianna on her Spanish. Those last six to eight weeks before arriving in Hispaniola could be crucial. I found out just yesterday that my guy was offered a better job, and he is reneging on our agreement."

"Send me," I said.

"What!"exclaimed James. No way, my friend, we can't ask you to do that."

"You didn't," I countered. "I volunteered for the job. Tianna already knows me, and we work well together. Plus, you know with my sailing skills and reputation, any captain would be thrilled to have me working on his ship in case of an emergency. There is no way that I would not be welcomed on the ship."

"I have never been on a slave ship before," said Maria, "But I am told that they are gruesome. I have even heard that ships carrying slaves can be smelled by other ships on the sea. Are you sure you are wanting to subject yourself to that?"

"I am sure that I don't want to, but I feel I need to do something. I promised myself that there is nothing that I wouldn't do to help prevent Fruga and Tianna from being seperated."

We discussed the idea back and forth, but in the end I prevailed. A week later I was on a ship headed to the Americas once again.

I remembered Maria's words about the stench of a slave trip as I approached the "King Ferdinand", the ship on which Fruga and Tianna would be brought to Hispaniola. The first of the supplies were being hauled on board as I checked in, the slaves were to be the last items loaded. People were not even on the boat, and already it stunk from its last voyage. Before helping to load crates, I took the time to look over the boat. It was the first slave transport that I had ever seen. It was a large galleon and I was grateful that it was not a Carrack, which they had started using once again to be able to transport even more slaves at a time.

The ship was outfitted with a special "slave hold" that was built below the deck. It spanned the entire length of the ship but was only chest high, an adult had to duck to walk through it. At the back of the hold was another set of steps that led to a supply room. The supply room had a second door that led down to the lower level of the galleon. This is where James arranged to have me assigned. My job was to be in charge of the supplies, to guard them from greedy crewmen, and to ration the food so that we did not run out. My cot was actually set up in the room right in front of the door, making it impossible for any thief to enter without waking me. As predicted, the captain of the ship, who I knew, was happy to have an able minded "backup" on board,

Finally, the slaves were led onto the ship. It was "all men on deck" to help make sure that none of the slaves broke away and dove overboard. The slaves were then led into the holding deck, beginning with the women and children, followed by the men, where they were then shackled by chains on the floor. I was shocked by the number of slaves that they crammed into the hold. If they stood they had one arms-length between them. To lay down, however, they were almost touching. As they entered, it was my job, as one of the few crew men who could do numbers, to write down the numbers that were branded into each slave's back or shoulder, unless he or she was rebellious; in which case they were often branded on the face. I remembered that Maria spent many nights checking enslaved people's brands for signs of infections.

It wasn't long after the ship was loaded that we headed out to sea. I remembered my last voyage to the New World with Christopher Columbus and the Pinzon brothers. I remembered the feeling of excitement and anticipation for our great adventure into the unknown. I felt nothing of the kind now. All that I felt was sadness for proud, innocent, and lovely people, who had been savagely ripped away from their families and were now being separated from the land they loved and the only home they had ever known.

As the days and nights passed the already deplorable conditions for the enslaved people worsened. The stench became nauseating and, because no air traveled through the hold, the heat made life unbearable, many slaves died and were unceremoniously thrown overboard. Sometimes if a slave became too sick, and it was feared that he or she might not die, but be too sick to sell, he or she would simply be thrown overboard while still alive. That way insurance could be collected. It was normal for twenty to thirty percent of the slaves shipped not to survive the crossing which was known as the middle passage. Sometimes that number rose to almost fifty percent. That is why they packed as many of the slaves on board as they could. Slaves died of dysentery, smallpox, or mere misery. Sometimes, preferring death to misery, slaves would choose not to eat, prompting guards to whip them severely and force food down their throats.

Men were allowed on deck once or twice a week and encouraged, often by a whip, to dance for exercise. Women were allowed to be on deck more often, but being on deck made them susceptible to sexual harassment or even rape. A ship's doctor was on board to try to keep the casualties to an "acceptable" number.

I checked in with Fugra and Tianna as often as I could during the day, but it broke my heart to see them suffering so much with very little that I could do for them. The night guards were two young teen-age boys who could care less about anything and were easily bribed. For a real each, which Maria and Julius gave me for the trip, I was able to bribe them to allow Fugra and Tianna to stay with me at night in the stockroom. I can't imagine what unspeakable things they must have thought that I was doing to them in that room by myself, although the truth was that the worse torture that I was subjecting them to was the task of learning Spanish verbs. After our lesson for the evening, I would let Fugra and Tianna share my cot, while I slept on some blankets on the other side of some supplies. The stench, moaning, and crying from the next room made sleeping difficult, but it was much better than being in the hold itself. We were sure to wake them up and get them back before the change of guard in the morning.

Finally, after what seemed like an eternity, the ship pulled into the dock and the trip was over. For me the nightmare was through, but for the enslaved people on board it was quite possible that the nightmare would be less horrific than the day that followed. I could only hope and pray that Fugra and Tianna would be pressed into service as house slaves, and would remain together.

CHAPTER THIRTY-SIX

"All feel justified. To find truth one must consider that he is wrong."

ALFRED LANCE CONRAD

After CookE had finished his story, Diego and Ferdinand remained quiet for a while, both caught up in thought. "That is an amazing story," Ferdinand finally said. "Do you still see Maria and her family?'

"Absolutely," replied CookE. "I eventually moved to Sierra Leone, and now call it home. When I am not at sea, I am working with Maria, trying to teach other young enslaved people how to speak Spanish. Maria chooses who I am to help, but it is usually someone young and bright, because young people pick up languages better than older adults. It is usually a girl, because girls have better chances of being bought for house slaves than do boys. For a while, I stayed in Maria and Julius' extra room, and they would be happy to have let me continue to live there, but I didn't want to impose and I value my own independence, so I found a place of my own. I rent a small apartment above a bakery. I still go to dinner at their house at least once a week, usually on Sundays."

"So you continue to work with the slaves, but you just don't sail on the same ship?"said Diego quizzically.

"That is right," answered CookE. "I still work with the enslaved people while they are in the compound, by doing a number of things, but mostly teaching Spanish. I will continue to keep an inventory as they enter the ships, but other than that, I refuse to have anything to do with them while on the sea. It was just too difficult for me the first time."

Something about CookE's story gnawed at Diego. It wasn't that he didn't believe CookE, he had grown to trust the man, but something just didn't quite fit. He was about to ask him about it, when Ferdinand chimed in, "How can people ever justify enslaving other human beings? How could anyone think that is okay?"

"Those are great questions and the same ones that I asked after my experience. I didn't have the answers so I turned to someone tremendously smarter than I. I asked Fr. Pablo. "

"Who is Fr. Pablo?"asked Diego.

"He is the finest priest that I have ever known. He is holy, smart, brave and compassionate, and the best part is that you will meet him when we arrive. Fr. Pablo comes down from the mission that he runs to trade food that he grows for the few items that they need which they cannot provide for themselves, like some types of medicine and a few other things."

"So what did Fr. Pablo say when you asked him about how people justify slavery?"asked Ferdinand getting the conversation back on track.

"Well," started CookE, "He explained that slavery itself is not new, The Greeks, Romans, and as we know, the Egyptians all had slaves. Throughout written human history slavery existed. In fact the native people of the Americas had their own slaves before they were conquered by us Europeans. However, throughout history people have never found the need to justify it, because slavery was just considered part of the spoils of war. The Greeks even offered to sell the slaves back after the war was over."

"But the situation today is different. These slaves cannot be considered the spoils of war, because they were in no war. They were simply living their lives the best that they could."

Interjected Diego.

"That is exactly what Fr. Pablo says,"continued CookE, " this is indeed a different situation. Now these men, women and children are being taken simply because it makes financial sense to take them. It is also the first time that we know of people are being chosen for enslavement because of the color of their skin. As we all know, people's consciences will not allow them to do things just because it makes them lots of money, so they find ways to justify what they are doing."

"Fr Pablo explained that this is done in many ways,"continued CookE. First they try to convince people that the black people are inferior and therefore not entitled to the same treatment as white people. Some will even go so far as to suggest that slavery is good for the enslaved, because the are incapable of taking care of themselves. Some will turn to science and find scientists who say that the black person's brain is actually less developed and even smaller than the white man's. This is done even though they do not back up the theory with any evidence whatsoever. Fr. Pablo even says that some will misinterpret the Bible in order to justify slavery. They profess that God created each of us to live out the roles that God has ordained for each of us, and God has created some people to be slaves."

"Obviously, none of these claims are based on anything factual and were invented to make people feel better about themselves by justifying their actions,"said CookE. "Fr. Pablo believes that the greater the atrocities that have to be justified, the more ridiculous the justifications. I certainly believe that to be true."

CHAPTER THIRTY-SEVEN

"Nothing weighs on us so heavily as a secret.

– JEAN DE LA FONTAINE

The next day, while they worked, Diego was quite upset. He was sure that there was a piece of CookE's story that just didn't quite fit. It wasn't so much the missing piece that was bothering him, it was the fact that CookE was concealing something important. Diego was hurt, because he thought throughout the weeks that they had worked together that a strong trust had developed between CookE and the two friends. Was he mistaken?

As always, he shared his feelings with Ferdinand. 'I just don't get it," said Diego,"If CookE doesn't even sail on the same ship as the slaves, why would he go at all. I understand that he might not be able to sail on the same ship because it is too difficult, but why go? Why not stay in Sierra Leone? Wouldn't he be more useful there working with the enslaved people? I tell you, Ferdinand, there is something that he is not telling us."

After thinking for a while, Ferdinand said, "I see your point, but I have to believe that there is a logical reason. Like you, I feel that we have earned CookE's trust. Maybe there is just a piece of the puzzle that he forgot to tell us or that we just don't understand. Let's ask him tonight."

As Diego, Ferdinand, and CookE settled down in their usual spot that evening it was Diego that asked the question, "CookE, Ferdinand and I were wondering, why do you sail on ships all the way to the Americas that have no slaves, when your passion in life seems to be helping the enslaved? I mean we don't want to be too bold or overstep, but wouldn't your time best be served by staying in Sierra Leone and working there, instead of making the long journey over the sea?"

CookE looked at Diego and then at Ferdinand and shook his head and laughed to himself, "I should have known that you two were just too smart.: he said.

"You can trust us CookE," said Ferdinand.

"I do totally trust you," responded CookE, "You are the only two friends that I have felt comfortable with to tell my story as far as I have, but I can't tell it all because, well," CookE paused. "Let me try it this way. Diego, if Rosalie told you something important to her, something that if it got out could hurt her badly, and she asked you not to tell another soul, would you tell me? Would you even share the secret with Ferdinand?"

Diego thought for a moment, then he looked first at CookE and then at his best friend, "No," he said, "Sorry, I couldn't."

"I wouldn't want you to,"said Ferdinand.

"Me either," said CookE.

"Thank you, CookE,"said Diego. "We now understand and respect the position that you are in, and we won't push you to reveal your secret."

"Yes," added Ferdinand, "In fact we now respect you more than ever."

The rest of the evening and much of the remaining trip was spent with CookE relaying stories of his friends who continued to sail after Columbus' first voyage. The most interesting by far, were those stories from those who sailed with Hernan

Cortes and the city of Tenochititian. They described seeing Tenochititian for the first time as being breathtaking and unforgettable. They said it was unlike any European city that they had ever seen, with more people and an extremely advanced culture. Finally, they talked about how Cortes with just a few hundred men were able to conquer thousands of Aztec warriors and destroy the city with superior weapons,playing on its leader, Montezuma's superstitions, and aided by a devastating outbreak of smallpox.

As the days passed, Diego and Ferdinand almost forgot about the missing piece of Diego's story. Then on the last day before their landing in Hispaniola, with land in sight, fate intervened and the secret was revealed — all the pieces fell into place.

CHAPTER THIRTY-EIGHT

"There's nowhere you can be that isn't where you're meant to be."

JOHN LENNON

Miguel was extra excited as he came below deck to tend to the barrels, he had just spied the land ahead, and he had never even left his home town before this trip. He was jabbering about what he was going to do when they landed while he did his daily chores. As he worked and talked, Diego, Ferdinand, and CookE busily cleaned out the horses' stalls and prepared them to finally be unloaded and led ashore. Due to the outstanding care of CookE and his crew, not one horse was lost.

A huge ruckus occurred as Miguel in his excitement accidentally allowed a barrel fall to the floor. When Diego and Ferdinand looked up to see what had happened, they were relieved to see that it was only a barrel that had fallen, but the horses had been spooked, and the one in the stall CookE was cleaning reflexively kicked him. When they looked over to the stall, he was on the ground writhing in pain and holding his leg, which was obviously broken.

Miguel, Ferdinand, and Diego all rushed to CookE's aid. "I

am so sorry, I can't believe I did that,"cried Miguel who was stricken with horror for what his carelessness had caused.

CookE, through his pain, replied with as much composure as he could, "Not your fault, Miguel, it was an accident. It could have happened to anyone."

Ferdinand ran up to let the Captain know what had happened. When he heard, Captain Sanchez sent a few men down to help get CookE into his cot and signaled to one of the slave carrying ships to send their doctor over in one of the lifeboats.

CHAPTER THIRTY-NINE

"Courage is resistance to fear, mastery of fear, not absence of fear."

Mark Twain

The doctor confirmed the obvious, the leg was broken. The doctor then set CookE's leg using two flat pieces of wood and some cloth and ordered him to remain in bed. "It seems like it is a pretty clean break, and if you take care to rest it, you should heal pretty nicely,"he said. "Tomorrow when we dock, I will ask the Captain to have a couple of men, carry you to shore where you can enjoy some fresh air, but physical activity is absolutely forbidden."

Miguel volunteered to help Diego, and Ferdinand to pick up the slack with CookE injured. "Thank you Cooke answered, but he had a very worried look on his face."

That night after the work was finished, Diego and Ferdinand went in to check on CookE. "Sit down, boys, we have to talk," said CookE. "I have been thinking and praying all day about what to do, and finally I have decided that I need to tell you my entire story, including the part that I had left out. First I need you two to promise me two things."

"Sure said Diego," looking at Ferdinand who nodded his agreement.

"The first thing is, that I want you to acknowledge that I am not only trusting you with my life by telling you what is really going on — I have no problem doing that — I am also trusting you with James', Maria's, Fr. Pablo's and possibly Julius' and the kids' life as well."

"So acknowledged," responded Ferdinand, "You can absolutely trust us." Both Ferdinand and Diego exchanged nervous glances.

"The second assurance that I need from you is confirmation that you understand that once you know the situation that you will not feel compelled to help out. The choice will be totally yours, I nor anyone else would blame you or think any less of you regardless."

Both boys agreed.

"Well," began, "Do you remember the story of how I got involved with working with Tianna?"

"Of course we do," said Diego.

"Well the story is totally true up unto the conversation on Christmas night, at least as far as I knew it at the time. After I had volunteered to go on the ship instead of the guy James originally had, remember how Maria had some concerns, and that after some more discussion, I prevailed?

"Yes," said the boys at the same time.

"It was actually a pretty important discussion. She was concerned about my state of mind after what I had already endured, but her concerns ran much deeper. She was mainly concerned about that which I didn't know,"said CookE. "Maria and Julius were hesitant, but James assured them that I could be trusted so Maria opened up."

CHAPTER FORTY

Maria's Story

"The only thing necessary for evil to triumph is for good men to do nothing."

EDMUND BURKE

Maria started to explain, "I first got involved with working with enslaved people quite by accident. I was working a shift one day and a slaver bought in a young enslaved man who had been cut on the upper arm trying to resist capture. I cleaned and stitched his wound. I remember the man looked so hopeless that my heart ached for him, not for the injury that would heal, but for the scars that I knew he would carry that would not. I decided a few days later to check in on him and perhaps clean the wound and change the bandage. It was truly a life-changing experience. My eyes were opened."

I was so engrossed in her story that I merely nodded my understanding. She continued, "I was angry with myself for knowing that slavery was happening and allowing myself to believe that it had nothing to do with my family or me. I was angry with the slave traders, and the slave buyers. I was angry with the government for allowing such an atrocity. I was extremely angry with the Church. Why wasn't it speaking out loudly and condemning the practice? Weren't we supposed to be the hands and feet of Christ? At this time in history weren't these the least of His people?"

"I remember thinking," she continued, "I had to do something. My father taught me that it was important to stand up for what is right even when doing so meant standing alone. Luckily, I am married to Julius," she said smiling at her husband, "So I am never really standing alone. I started going to the compound in the evenings and tending to the sick and injured, while Julius took on all the extra responsibility of caring for the children every night."

"It is the least that I could do,"said Julius, "How often does a man get a chance to support his wife and help innocent people at the same time. I am just blessed to be a part of it in some way."

"After a while, however, it became clear that by tending to the slaves, I was also helping the slavers,"continued Maria. "We had to find a way to at least free some of them. We knew we could not free enough people to really adversely affect the slave trade, but we also knew that it would make a tremendous impact on the lives of those we could free. So Julius came with me one afternoon to study the compound's security in order to determine if freeing any of the slaves was possible."

"Well you saw the fence and the guards," interjected Julius, "It wasn't possible. At least it could not be done without great risk to us and the enslaved people. If we tried we would almost certainly have caused our children to be orphans and possibly subjected some of the slaves to cruel punishment, or even death."

"And besides,"added Maria. "Even if we were successful once, which is highly unlikely, we would certainly get caught the next time. We didn't want to help a handful of people one time, we wanted to continuously help a few people. That was when my genius brother stepped in with a fantastic plan,"she said nodding at James.

James then spoke up, "I had already made up my mind to

quit my job recruiting and assigning people to work on ships, because so many of the ships I assigned them to transported slaves. When my sister told me about her struggles of conscience and what she was trying to do, I had a better idea. Instead of quitting my job, I would use it to help free some of the enslaved people."

"That's why you were in the recruiting office, when I walked in!"interrupted Ferdinand. "You were not only friends with James, but you are accomplices with whatever this scheme is?" The pieces were finally beginning to fall into place.

CookE nodded, "It was apparent that security in the camp was far too tight for us to breach. It had to be, because the slavers were constantly on guard against internal insurrection or attack from slaves' friends and families on the outside. On the other side of the Atlantic, however, it was a different story. The feeling was that a group of enslaved people, who had just been ripped from their home and families and subjected to weeks of torment aboard a slave ship, were not ripe for rebellion. They were too broken to attempt an escape. Plus there would be no one in this unfamiliar foreign land to help them."

"So security in Hispaniola was much more lax which really worked to your advantage?"asked Diego.

"Yes, but the thing that really worked to our advantage was the sad fact that so many of the enslaved people died during the trip that the slavers really had no accurate idea of what slaves actually made the trip alive or even how many. Especially, if the men assigned with the responsibility of watching them were uneducated and could not count."

"And of course, they were uneducated and could not count," guessed Diego, "Because James only assigned people to the job who were uneducated and could not count."

Ferdinand and Diego's minds were beginning to see more and more clearly as CookE laid out the story. "So who chooses who you will save?"asked Ferdinand.

"That unenviable job falls to Maria," said CookE. "Unfortunately, we can only save six to eight people at a time. Maria always chooses a family unit that has somehow managed to stay at least partially together. In the case of Fugra and Tianna, we were also saving Fugra's sister, her sister"s husband, and four children."

"So you teaching Tianna how to speak Spanish wasn't really to increase her chances of being a house slave rather than a field worker?"asked Diego.

"Well it wasn't the primary reason anyway,"responded CookE. "If our plan didn't work, it would have been to her advantage to know Spanish, but the goal was for her not to end up being any kind of slave. We needed her to be able to speak enough Spanish to understand our plan and be able to explain it to her family. If there had to be a last minute change, we also needed a way that also could be communicated."

"So, you volunteered to go instead of the guy who backed out at the last minute because he got a better job offer?"asked Diego.

"Yes," replied CookE, "But of course he did not really get a better job offer, he just reevaluated the situation and thought that the risk was too high. I was actually a better fit anyway, because I have been sailing for a long time, and many people know and trust me. James said he would have asked me in the first place, but was afraid that it would have been too stressful on me after my ordeal with the Columbus voyage."

Ferdinand and Diego were getting excited the way people do when a difficult puzzle begins to unravel. "So once you got them to America, how did you steal them away from the slavers?"asked Diego.

"They didn't!"exclaimed Ferdinand, who was one step ahead of his friend at figuring out the scheme. "They were never with the slavers. You simply had them stay on the ship somewhere and turned in a count that was eight people less than the actual. When they counted bodies it was a match. No one came looking for the missing slaves, because no one knew there were any. Brilliant!"

CookE laughed, "And you two are pretty brilliant yourselves. It was pretty easy because everyone figured that, as soon as the slaves were able to leave the disgusting confines of the hold where they had been imprisoned, they would be eager to get out. No one thought that anyone would stay behind, and no one wanted to go check, because that would mean that they would have to enter the squalor. Besides the count matched, so what would be the point?"

"The plan worked without hardly a hitch," said CookE reminensing," the only slight issue was that one of the boys who were watching the slaves asked me if it weren't difficult for me to sail on a slave ship when I must have been against slavery. He reasoned that I had to be against slavery if I worked for their benefit while they were still in the compound. I gave him some flimsy reason, but it must have been good enough, because nothing ever came of it. After I shared this with James, Maria, and Julius it was decided that it would be best that in the future I not sail on the slave ships, because of my opposition to slavery. We could still accomplish the same with less suspicion as long as I agreed to do the inventory, which James made sure was always part of my job as the overall live cargo manager."

"All of this makes perfect sense now," exclaimed Diego, "But what about Fruga, Tianna and their family? Where did they go? How did you get them off the ship?"

"Well my young friends, those are very good questions, which lead me to the part that will involve you if you decide it is something that you want to do."

PART THREE

CHAPTER FORTY-ONE

The Mission

"Freedom lies in being bold."

ROBERT FROST

The ship was anchored in the harbor and the crew and cargo would be unloaded first thing in the morning. CookE had refused to accept an answer from either Diego or Ferdinand until they had time to think about the situation, what was to be gained as well as what they were risking.

"Are you thinking about whether or not you want to do this?"asked Ferdinand.

"No,"answered Diego, "I know I want to do it. You?"

"Same."answered Ferdinand, "But perhaps you should rethink it. Remember Rosalie is waiting for you back home to return and marry her."

"I am thinking about Rosalie, she is about all I think of since we started on this journey,"responded Diego. "What do you think she would want me to do if she were here?"

Ferdinand laughed quietly, "Point taken, if she were here she would not only want you to go, she would demand to go with us."

"Yep," said Diego, smiling,"That's my fiancé."

Changing the subject, Ferdinand said, "Wow, no wonder CookE has such a high opinion of Fr. Pablo. To think he risks his life to save and then care for so many people Christians and non-Christians alike. That is what I think being a Christian is like. Jesus said love your neighbor. He never said love your white neighbor or your Christian neighbor."

CookE had shared with the boys last night that he always had it prearranged that he got a two week holiday after they landed in Hispaniola to visit his friend Fr. Pablo. While he was gone, the cooks on the other boats took care of feeding the crew and stocking the ships for the return journey. On Fr. Pablo's journey from the mission to the encampment, he would always stop up the coast and hide a canoe, as was the arrangement between him and his good friend, James.

Fr. Pablo would trade his fresh goods for the supplies he needed, share a meal with CookE and a few of the captains, and then he and CookE, along with a couple of Fr. Pablo's helpers would head off to the mission with his supplies. When they reached the spot where the canoe was hidden, CookE would stop and wait. As soon as it grew dark enough and CookE was sure that the crew would be out around the campfire eating, drinking, and celebrating having arrived safely; CookE would paddle around to the other side of the ship. He then would tie up the canoe, retrieve the slaves still on board, slip on down with them to the canoe and paddle back to shore. Once on shore they would follow Fr. Pablo back up to the mission, reaching it just as morning was breaking. CookE explained that they had successfully followed this routine five times. If the boys were up for taking his spot, this would be the sixth time. Thirty-eight men, women, and children who would have been slaves were free because of these heroic efforts. Ferdinand and Diego were determined that after tomorrow night, there would be forty-six.

CHAPTER FORTY-TWO

'The purpose of life is not to be happy. It is to be useful, to be honorable, to be compassionate, to have it make some difference that you have lived and lived well."

RALPH WALDO EMERSON

After a restless night, Ferdinand and Diego rose before the dawn. They decided to begin this momentous day on their knees. Together they prayed the rosary to the Lady of the Pillar asking for her intercession. As they did so, both boys' thoughts were taken back to the night outside of Isabelle's house. After they finished their formal prayers, Ferdinand looked up and implored, "Isabelle, please watch over us and send angels to protect us." Then the two boys crossed themselves.

"Are you afraid?"asked Diego.

"Absolutely," responded Ferdinand, "You?"

"Absolutely."replied Diego.

Finally, whistles signaled the crew that it was time to get moving. It was a beautiful day and the sun was already warming the earth. The scenery was breathtaking. "America is certainly a beautiful place."said Diego, as he and Ferdinand walked down the ramp and touched ground for the first time in over a month.

CookE, who had already been helped ashore, laughed when he saw the two boys struggle to stand straight. "You don't have your land legs yet," he shouted it won't take long."

Cooke was sitting next to Captain Sanchez. "I was just telling the captain that you two were smart and good with numbers, and said that you would be glad to inventory the slaves as they were unloaded."said CookE.

"Thank you, boys,"said the Captain.

"I was also hoping that it would be okay if they went with Fr. Pablo in my place to help carry the supplies and visit the mission. It will give them a chance to go to mass, which is important to them,"said CookE.

"No problem," said Captain Sanchez, "as long as you are back in two weeks. We can wait for no one." The captain tipped his hat as he headed back toward the boats.

"How did you know that we would say yes?"asked Ferdinand after the captain had left.

"Is the answer yes?"asked CookE.

"Absolutely," said Diego.

CookE just smiled. "You boys better go and set out some food, breakfast will be on shore today. The slaves will be the last thing unloaded. Someone will call you when you need to take the inventory. Mufa, who is on the La Conquistador, the second ship on the right is ten years old. He picked up Spanish quickly. He will be scared when he sees you, because he is expecting me. Say the word, 'zebra', this is a code word which will let him know that I sent you. He will be with his mom and dad, three sisters and his aunt and uncle."

"Can we get you anything before we go?"asked Ferdinand.

"No, thank you," said CookE, and the two boys turned to unload breakfast.

After breakfast had been served and the leftovers packed away, Ferdinand and Diego, began to help the rest of the crew unpack the remaining cargo, "Look," exclaimed Ferdinand as he pointed up the beach at a man dressed in white along with three young men who were each leading two mules overloaded with all sorts of fruits and vegetables. "I bet that is Fr. Pablo."

His hunch was confirmed when the man directed his three assistants to bring the mules over to the trade manager while he stopped to meet with CookE.

CookE noticed the boys looking their way and waved them over. "Hello, I am Fr. Pablo" he said extending his hand in greeting when the boys arrived. "CookE tells me some great things about you two. He says that you are the finest assistants with whom he has ever sailed."

"You should hear what he has told us about you."said Diego, extending his hand.

"A true pleasure to meet you, Fr.Pablo," said Ferdinand as he shook the priest's hand.

"Are you sure you guys are up for this?"asked Fr. Pablo looking at each of the boys in turn. "I would go myself, but I have too many people depending on me at the mission."

"Absolutely, we are," said Diego.

"Are you afraid?"

"Absolutely, we are," said Ferdinand.

"Both answers are exactly what I hoped to hear,"said Fr. Pablo. "It means that you are brave, but not fool hardy. Please know that you will both be in my prayers."

"Thank you," said both boys in unison.

"Why don't you boys, go and put out dinner?"said CookE. "Then it will be time to unload the enslaved people. The boys will have to stay and take the inventory, and then you should all be able to head out together,"he added to Fr. Pablo.

"Sounds like a plan," said Diego, as he and Ferdinand turned to set up the food.

After lunch Miguel was left to clean up and put things away, as the two boys were called to take inventory of the enslaved people. Diego, would check off the brand number as Ferdinand read them aloud. On the bottom of the page were tally marks for each one of the slaves who had died and had been discarded overboard. In each case the number of slaves exiting plus the number of tally marks equaled the number of slaves that began the forced journey, except of course when they came to the La Conquistador. The fix was easy as the boys simply added eight tallies to the sheet. Everything matched as far as the slavers were concerned. They thanked Ferdinand and Diego for the assistance and headed off in the opposite direction.

The boys then joined Fr. Pablo and his assistants who were standing by the mules that had been unloaded and loaded again. In turn each boy hugged CookE and bid him farewell. “See you in two weeks,”said CookE, “Go with God.”

CHAPTER FORTY-THREE

"You have to take risks. You will only understand the miracle of life fully when you allow the unexpected to happen."

PAULO COELHO

As the group trudged through the path they were definitely on a steady incline. Ferdinand and Diego were enthralled with the wonder of the forest around them. They had never seen anything to compare to the lushness of the vegetation or the colorful birds, lizards, and other animals they encountered. Finally after about fifteen or twenty minutes, Fr. Pablo veered to his right and led Diego and Ferdinand down through the forest to a spot between two steep drops, where one could descend by sitting on their butts and easing their way down. Diego and Ferdinand followed Fr. Pablos's lead down to the sea. When he reached the shore he lifted a branch to reveal a canoe that was tied up out of sight.

"Here you go boys,"said Fr. Pablo. "In about two and a half hours it should be dark enough for you to set out, and everyone should be on shore enjoying the first day feast. See that funny looking twisted tree just down a little bit."

The boys nodded.

"Look for that on your way back," said Fr. Pablo, "That will let you know when it is time to pull ashore. Then just climb up the bank and follow the trail all the way up to the mission. The mission is at the top of the hill so you can not miss it." Then he blessed the boys and headed back up the hill."

Ferdinand and Diego, settled down in the canoe and waited. While they waited they prayed. Then both boys became very quiet. "What are you thinking about," asked Diego, finally breaking the silence after what seemed an eternity.

"I am thinking about how difficult the waiting is for us, but how much more difficult it must be for Mafu and his family sitting hidden somewhere in the squalor hoping that we can come to their rescue."

"That is just one of the many things I love about you, said Diego. Here we find ourselves about to embark on a very dangerous mission, and your mind is on the plight of others and not yourself. That is why you and Isabelle were such a great couple."

Diego smiled, "Do you think it is time yet?"

"Let's say a quick rosary to the Lady of the Pillar, and then head out," replied Ferdinand.

The boys were not accustomed to paddling a canoe, so it took a few minutes to get the hang of things, but once they did, it was pretty smooth sailing. The moon was bright that night with only a few clouds in the sky, which had both its advantages and disadvantages. The boys were able to easily chart a path to the back side of the La Conquistador, but also it meant there was a brief moment when they could be spotted from the shore if someone happened to be looking in that direction.

The boys held their breath as they approached the moonlit area where they would be susceptible, but as they approached one of the few clouds in the night sky drifted in front of the moon. The boys just looked at each other in amazement. "My best friend once told me that God often works miracles in ways that often appear to be coincidence," said Diego. I believe he is right."

"Thank you, Mother Mary," said Ferdinand as he crossed himself.

Diego had no problem scaling the back side of the La Conquistador and threw a rope ladder down to Ferdinand. They both gagged as soon as they opened the door to the slave hold. It took three times before they were able to stick even their heads inside without having to vomit. Finally, holding their breath, they looked in and saw nothing. In a voice a little louder than a whisper, Ferdinand said, "Zebra."

Out of the shadows emerged a young boy, followed by seven other people who looked and smelled like they had been through hell itself. "It's okay," said Diego. "We are friends of CookE, he got hurt and couldn't come, but we are here to help. Come with us."

Even in the dark they could see the expression of relief on their faces. Mafu, tell your family that the canoe is just on the side of the boat and that you should all come with us. Mafu related the message and the group headed up into the night air. Diego descended the rope ladder first, mafu followed, and then his three sisters. The adults were so weak and disoriented that Ferdinand had to help them onto the ladder and Diego assisted them getting off into the canoe. Finally, Ferdinand climbed down and the boys pushed off. The newly freed people started to cry with joy as the boys paddled them to freedom. "Thank you, thank you, thank you,' they said repeating the few words in Spanish that they knew.

With the added weight in the canoe, Diego and Ferdinand had to reacquaint themselves with the best ways to steer and paddle the canoe. As they figured it out the craft increased in speed. The small cloud continued to cover the moon, so it appeared that they made the rescue without a problem, but when they got to the coast they were past the tree, before they realized it. They tried to steer the canoe around, but found that their canoeing skills were not up to the task. They began to panic, when suddenly a head popped up in front of them and someone handed them a rope..

Ferdinand was unsure what he should do, who the person was who handed them the rope, or if they were in trouble. So he took the rope and started to pull. The canoe turned direction and started to be pulled to shore. Diego and the two men joined Ferdinand, and soon the canoe was back on shore right where it was supposed to be. After they were on shore, Diego and Ferdinand watched bewildered as a young girl about their age emerged from the water. "Hello," she said with a beautiful smile, "My name is Tianna."

CHAPTER FORTY-FOUR

"Fight for the things that you care about, but do it in a way that will lead others to join you."

RUTH BADER GINSBURG

'You must be Diego, and you must be Ferdinand,"said Tianna nodding at each of the boys respectively. Fr. Pablo told me about you, and also said that you might have trouble finding the right place to dock, as you are unfamiliar with the shoreline. I tied the rope to the tree and was ready to jump in and bring the other end to you if it was necessary, which it apparently was."

"Thank you so very much," replied Ferdinand. "I am not sure what we would have done if we had passed the tree.'

"I believe that you probably would have figured it out, but it is better that you didn't have to," said Tianna, downplaying what she had just done for the group. "Fr. Pablo says you two are friends of CookE and that he trusts you. Any friend of CookE's is a friend of mine,"she said. "I am so sorry that I will not get a chance to visit with him this time."

Ferdinand laughed a little to himself,"You know," he said,"CookE talked a lot about you, about how special and smart you are, and how he taught you Spanish. I imagined you as he told us the story, so in my mind I pictured you as he described you when you two met. I was surprised when you told us who you were."

Tianna laughed, "Yes I grew quite a bit in the last eight years."

"Is it cold?"asked Diego referring to the water dripping off of Tianna.

"No," she answered, "The water feels great. It is very refreshing and works wonders for cleansing the body," she said putting emphasis on the word 'cleansing."

Diego laughed, "Are you trying to tell us that we need cleansing?"he asked.

"Actually," she responded, " I was trying very hard not to have to tell you," she smiled.

With that Diego and Ferdinand laughed and jumped in the water, and the rest of the group followed, even Tianna. They laughed and splashed and rejoiced in the water. At least for the moment they were happy, and free. Tianna was right, the water was refreshing, and although they did not have soap, the water did help to watch away most of the dirt, the grime, and the stench of the past seven weeks.

As they sat on the shore drying off, Ferdinand asked Mafu to introduce his family after he introduced Tianna, Diego and himself to him. When Mafu was told that Tianna was the first student that CookE taught Spanish, he felt a common bond between them. "CookE, is a great man," he said, if it wasn't for him and Maria and now you all, I don't know what would have happened to my family, but I know it would have been horrible."

"Shhh," said Tianna, looking around, "I think I hear," but she wasn't able to finish her sentence before four rugged men emerged from the bushes behind them.

Everyone quickly got to their feet. "Hey Manuel,"said the apparent leader and biggest guy in the group, "These here are definitely not the escaped slaves that we have been hunting, but why not, they'll do, after all a slave is a slave. Boss man will be fine if we bring these back instead. Only five escaped, if we bring back nine, we may even get a bonus."

Diego stepped forward, " No way, these are our escaped slaves, and we are bringing them back to our compound. Get out of our way."

"Well," said the big man, "They may have been your escaped slaves, but you have one problem. You see there are four of us, and everyone of us is much bigger than either of you two. So now they are our escaped slaves."

"Hey look here," said one of the other men. "All these slaves are scrawny and look like hell, they must be new arrivals, but this one looks nice and healthy," he said walking towards Tianna. "I think I had better take a look and see just how healthy she " He didn't get a chance to finish the sentence when a left hook from Ferdinand caught him squarely in the chin knocking him to the ground unconscious.

After a few seconds in shock, Diego ran directly at the biggest of the scoundrels tackling him to the ground. His mind was racing, "I have to get this guy out quickly he thought, despite Ferdinand's surprising left hook, he knew he wasn't a fighter. He didn't know about Tianna, but he knew that Mufa's dad and uncle were much too weak from the voyage to do much damage. Unfortunately, it took him longer than he wanted to get the better of the big guy. Finally he was able to knock him out, and jumped to his feet ready to take on the next opponent. However, when he looked around all four of the men lay prone on the ground, everyone was staring at Ferdinand with surprise. Ferdinand was stooping over offering Tianna a hand up.

"Oh my goodness," said Mufa, "that was amazing!"

"What happened?"asked Diego, "I was too busy taking on that one guy, I didn't see what was happening."

"After Ferdinand punched the creep I took a run at the guy next to him, but he quickly knocked me down," said Tianna. "Ferdinand took care of him and the other one on his own. I never saw anyone fight so well."

Diego looked at his friend, "What? How? How did I not know you could fight."

"My dad started teaching me to fight when I was very, very, young," said Ferdinand. "Just in case I would ever have to do it. I never told you, for the same reason I never told anyone. Being able to fight is not something that I hold in high esteem. I was always more proud of my ability to avoid fighting than my ability to fight. That is why you never knew I could fight, and to be honest with you, I prefer you never had to find out."

"So all those times when Juan was mean to you...?'said Diego, his voice trailing off.

"I didn't believe and still don't believe that because someone teases you or bullies you is a reason to fight. I believe that Jesus meant what he said when he told us to turn the other cheek, when we can. I just didn't see how it was possible in this situation. If I am able to live the rest of my life without striking another man, that would be a good thing."

"Like I said before, I will never understand you,"said Diego.

"Actually," said Ferdinand, "The fact that I have the ability to fight is the only secret about me that you have not known for a long time."

"Well," said Diego, "Thank God for your secret. Without it, we would all be in a lot of trouble."

"Speaking of trouble," said Tianna, "We better get a move on it before these guys wake up."

CHAPTER FORTY-FIVE

"He is no fool who gives what he cannot keep to gain that which he cannot lose."

JIM ELIOT

It was early in the morning, when the group reached the "Santa Maria Mission," It was situated on top of a hill, with its back overlooking a drop to the ocean. Even before the sun fully lit the earth, Diego and Ferdinand could tell that the scenery had to be magnificent. As the group climbed the steps dug into the hillside that led to the end of their destination, they were all struggling to make it.

When they reached the door it was opened by Fr. Pablo and a woman to whom Tianna ran and the two embraced. "Hello, he said to Mafu and his family. I am Fr. Pablo. Welcome to the Santa Maria Mission. You have already met Tianna, and this is her mother, Fugra. We look forward to getting to know all of you and showing you your new home, but I know that you must be exhausted. Fugra and Tianna will show you to your huts and I will take Diego and Ferdinand to theirs, please sleep as late as you can. Your bodies will need it. We will talk in the morning." Mafu translated the message for his family and they headed off with Fugra and Tianna again repeating the words, "Thank you, thank you, thank you."

Fr. Pablo then led the boys to their hut. As they walked

Ferdiand remarked, "So I see this is the Santa Maria Mission?"

"Yes," said Fr. Pablo, The ship the Santa Maria brought much pain and suffering to many people of this beautiful land. It is my hope that the Santa Maria Mission brings nothing but love and healing, and be a much more fitting tribute to our Holy Mother."

"I love the idea," replied Ferdinand as they reached their hut.

The sun was shining bright when Diego and Ferdinand awoke later that day. "I wonder what time it is?"said Ferdinand, stretching.

"No idea," said Diego, "boy did I sleep well."

"Me too," said Ferdinand, "I slept so well I didn't even hear you snoring like a bear."

"Ha," said Diego, sitting on the edge of his bed. "Can you believe that we are here and what we have done?"

"It is hard to believe, so much has happened."

"Rosalie won't believe it,"said Diego with a smile.

"What part won't she believe?"asked Ferdinand. " The part about CookE and his amazing stories, or almost being capsized, or us saving eight people from slavery?"

""No,"responded Diego, "She will believe all that."

"Then what?"asked Ferdiand.

"That you can fight!"declared Diego laughing.

Ferdinand responded by playfully throwing his shoe at him. Diego ducked and the shoe hit Fr. Pablo who had just opened the door. "So, sorry Father, said Ferdinand, are you okay."

Fr. Pablo just laughed, "Yes," he replied, "Didn't know I was entering a war zone. I just came in to check on you guys. I see that you are awake. Mafu and his family are also awake."

"Are they going to be okay?"asked Diego.

"Yes, in time they will be physically okay any way. Right now they are suffering from malnutrition and dehydration, but Florencia will nurse them back to health. Florencia is the closest thing we have to a doctor here at the mission, but she is excellent. She knows what herbs and grains are good for all sorts of cures. She is most worried about the aunt because she is carrying the baby, but she thinks both mother and baby will survive. Thank you, Jesus."

"Oh my goodness," said Diego.

"We did not know she was pregnant,"said Ferdinand.

"Yes, boys, you did not save eight people from slavery last night. You saved nine,"said Fr. Pablo. "How does it feel?"

Diego and Ferdinand looked at each other. "It feels wonderful, greater than anything I ever imagined," said Diego.

"No matter what else you accomplish during your lifetimes, most people will not have accomplished nearly so much as you already have. I am proud of you boys."

"Thank you, Fr. Pablo," answered Ferdinand, " We are so grateful for having had the opportunity. Did you hear that we did encounter a problem last night?"

"Yes, Tianna told us all about it,"said, Fr. Pablo,"She told me that you, Diego, told them that you were slavers that had just recaptured them. Quick thinking. She also told me about how brave you both were. Tianna is very special to me, she really had to beg me to let her go help you last night, because I was afraid for her. I will never forget what you did for her as well."

"Well we were certainly glad to have her with us. We would definitely have missed the docking point if she was not there,"said Ferdinand. "So you don't think that those men would come looking for us here? We would not want to bring trouble with us."

"Not a chance,"said Fr. Pablo. "Even if they knew where to find you, which they wouldn't because of your quick thinking, they would never come here. This whole mission is part of the Catholic Church and therefore everyone here has safe sanctuary. Not even the lowest scoundrel would dare to infringe upon the protection of the Church. It just would not be wise. So why don't you guys come down to the dining hall? You have to be hungry and Fugra has held back some food for you. Afterwards, Tianna and I will take you on a tour of the place."

CHAPTER FORTY-SIX

"The best way to find yourself is to lose yourself in the service of others."

MAHATMA GANDHI

The food was delicious, it was such a long time since Diego and Ferdinand ate something that was fresh that they took their time enjoying every bite. After they were finished eating, they cleaned up after themselves and thanked Fugra.

As they walked out of the hut, they found Fr. Pablo and Tianna waiting for them. The four talked as they walked around the huts which were similar to those that CookE described belonging to the Taino that Columbus and his men encountered. When they reached the back side of the mission they all stopped. The view was simply amazing. "I have been part of this Mission here now for almost fifteen years," said Fr. Pablo, "Yet I never get tired of looking at this view. I often come here to pray. Here, I feel so close to God, it is wonderful." They all stopped for several minutes of reverent silence, enjoying the view of the sea, before continuing their tour.

"So you have been ministering here for almost fifteen years?"asked Ferdinand as a way of starting the conversation.

"Yes," said Fr. Pablo, "Most of my original flock were Taino seeking shelter. They were families who had lost their father to enslavement or death at the hands of the Europeans or mothers and or children whose families were wiped out by smallpox or other diseases to which they had no immunity. As you can see there are still a number of Taino here, but as the years went by, and the few Taino that were not annihilated were no longer allowed to be slaves, our demographic has largely changed towards more Africans. Thanks largely to the fine work of CookE, Maria, James and even Julius who does so much behind the scenes in support. You will even notice some Spaniards who have found themselves widowed or orphaned. We don't care. All are God's children. All are welcomed."

"Christians and non-Christians alike?" asked Ferdinand.

Fr. Pablo took a second to answer. "Yes, he finally said, "But I would appreciate it if you did not mention that part to anyone when you return to Spain."

"You mean the Church does not know that you do not require conversion to help people?"asked Ferdinand.

"They really don't know what I do out here, I don't suppose,"said Fr. Pablo. "To be honest I think that they were just very glad to see me go so far away. I guess I am just not very good at keeping my opinions to myself, and there is much that is going on and has gone on with the Church that I just don't think is right, especially with the Inquisition and treatment of the Moors and Jews."

"Yet you continue to serve the Church, faithfully?' asked Diego.

"Absolutely," replied Fr. Pablo. "How can I not? The Church is the Body of Christ, even if some of its members are not following in Jesus' footsteps as they are called to do."

"That has to be hard," said Diego.

"It can be," said Fr. Pablo, "But we have a great example to follow."

"You mean Jesus, right?"said Ferdinand.

"Of course, when Jesus walked the earth His Church had lost its way. It was putting the law over love and its leaders were putting their glory over God's glory. He came to be the light to show us the way. They rejected him and even tried to kill him several times, but he remained faithful, because he recognized the church of his time as the house of his Father. As our Church is the Body of Christ, we must follow his example."

"Wow," said Diego, "That is a wonderful way to look at things. Thanks for the insight, but do you ever get lonely or feel that you are trying to accomplish so much on your own."

"Not at all," said Fr. Pablo. "I am not even close to being the only Catholic priest following Jesus' footsteps, or at least trying the best I can. Priests and lay people are doing it all the time all over the world, and while things in the Church might seem bleak, the Spirit will always prevail. I have a good friend named Inigo who just became a priest a short time ago. I think he goes by Ignatius now, but he and I correspond all of the time. His ideas are really refreshing, and I believe that he and others will be instrumental in moving the Church in the right direction. As he put it in his last letter, 'If our church is not marked by caring for the poor, the oppressed, the hungry, we are guilty of heresy.' We will always serve the Church as the Body of Christ, but out of love for Christ and His Church, we must always keep its leaders accountable as we also keep each other accountable -- always remembering that we are all sinners in need of saving.".

The next stop was the gardens where all types of food were being grown. The men and women working in the gardens, stopped when they saw us and waved. "It looks like the gardens are very healthy," said Diego. "So how does it work? Does each family get a piece of land to farm?"

"No," said Fr. Pablo, "We are set up like the early Christians in the Acts of the Apostles. Everything belongs to God, no one actually owns anything. The farmers grow food for everyone, the fishermen fish for everyone, the hunters hunt for everyone, there are women who sew clothes for the entire village, and carpenters who make homes and furniture for whoever needs it, and so on. Of course others earn their keep by teaching the children, which is what Tianna, would normally be doing, but we gave her the day off after her escapade last night."

"Seems like a wonderful system," said Ferdinand. "Where

would you like us to work?"

"Work?,"asked Fr. Pablo, "You are not here to work, this is a break for you. You deserve it after what you did for Mafu and his family. You really came through."

"Please, Fr. Pablo, we want to help," said Ferdinand.

"You sure?," asked Fr. Pablo.

"Absolutely," answered Diego, "I would like to learn how some of these plants are grown anyway. There is a parcel of land behind the orphanage at home, that I would like to plant some things in for the kids there. Not only could they use the food, but it would be good for teaching them responsibility and how to grow things themselves."

"Excellent,"said Fr. Pablo, "You can start tomorrow. Anthony will be a great teacher and very grateful for the help. Where do you think you would like to work, Ferdinand?"

"Well, if Tianna could use the help, I would love to work in the school."

Tianna smiled, "I would love to have help, if it is okay with Fr. Pablo."

"Absolutely," responded Fr. Pablo,"Then it is all set."

"Figures that you would end up in school," remarked Diego looking at Ferdinand, "Super genius here had the highest marks in school his last three years, but I am the real brains of the group,"said Diego, teasing his friend.

"The guy comes up with two good ideas, and his head is as big as the moon, ." Ferdinand teased back.

Fr. Pablo said, "Okay we already know about him coming up with the idea of you two being slavers to fool the real slavers, but what was the other one to which you are referring?"

Ferdinand recounted the scheme that Diego, Rosalie, and Isabelle had carried out against Juan as retribution for what he had done. By the time he was finished Fr. Pablo and Tianna were hysterically laughing. "You four must have been quite a group! Are you all still great friends?"

"Rosalie and I are engaged," replied Diego,"I am counting the days until we can be together again. Ferdinand and Isabelle had plans to marry but sadly, Isabelle died of consumption."

"So sorry," said Fr. Pablo and Tianna simultaneously.

"It was hard on us all,"said Ferdinand, "We all loved her. She was very special."

'You must miss her terribly," sad Tianna looking at Ferdinand.

"I do miss not having her with me in person," said Ferdiand, "But sometimes I can still feel her with me. I guess that sounds kind of strange."

"It doesn't seem strange to me at all," replied Tianna, "I still feel my father with me often, even after eight years. In my culture, the feeling of connectedness with our ancestors is part of the fabric of our lives. It is even more important to the Taino. I mean no disrespect Fr. Pablo, but to the Christians that I know it seems like they have faith that they will be with loved ones in the next life, but I don't get as much of a sense that they believe that they are with them in the here and now."

"That's an interesting observation," said Fr. Pablo, "You might be right, but our belief in the 'Communion of Saints' certainly tells us that there is a connectedness between all people who are in God's graces."

CHAPTER FORTY-SEVEN

"Courage is the power to let go of the familiar."

RAYMOND LINDQUIST

The first eight days at the mission flew by quickly. The boys would rise early, wash up and take a walk before breakfast.. Often, Tianna joined them on their walk. After breakfast, Diego headed out to the fields, and Tianna and Ferdinand headed to the school.

The midday meal was served at noon followed by the customary siesta. Then work and classes resumed. School was dismissed late afternoon, and the other workers remained in the fields until early evening.

After the children were dismissed from school, Ferdinand and Tianna would spend time preparing the next days' lesson. The two made a good team, Ferdinand was more capable in the core areas of math, science, and grammar, while Tianna flourished in the knowledge of local customs, art, music and in general the most effective way to teach languages. The two soon began to form a bond and started to learn from each other.

Right before supper, Fr. Pablo would celebrate a daily mass in the small chapel. Ferdinand and Diego were always in attendance. After mass and the evening meal the whole community would gather around a campfire. People would take turns telling stories-both funny and scary -- and engage in much singing and dancing, until it was time to retire into their own small hut for the night.

On Saturday. Diego, Ferdinand and Tianna engaged in a game of team tag against a whole slew of children, a game affectionately dubbed the "Giants vs. the Wee People." No one kept score and everyone had much fun. After the game, Tianna showed the boys a path down from the drop off at the back of the mission, which led down to the ocean. "This is still part of the mission, said Tianna, "So we are safe."

The three spent most of the rest of the day relaxing in the sun. They swam, collected shells, made sand castles, napped and talked. Tianna told the boys all about life in Africa, and the boys told her all about life in Spain. "You know what is strange?"asked Ferdinand after a while.

"What?"said Tianna, smiling.

"We are so different. We come from different parts of the world, our beliefs are different, our customs are different, and even the color of our skin is different. But after spending less that a week with you, Tianna, it seems to me that we are so much more alike than we are different," said Ferdinand.

"That is so true,"agreed Diego.

"Yes," agreed Tianna, "I believe that if more people throughout the world, understood what you just said, Ferdinand, we would all live in a better place."

After mass and evening meal, Fr. Pablo and Ferdinand went for a walk at Ferdinand's request. In the week that Ferdinand had been at the mission his trust and respect for Fr. Pablo and his ministry grew immensely, he figured that Fr. Pablo would be a good person from whom to seek counsel. He found that he could confide easily with Fr. Pablo. He told him about his efforts to discern whether or not he was called to become a priest. He talked about his life in Zaragoza. He talked about his faith, his beliefs, his love for Isabelle and how that had changed the direction of his life. He even told him about Fr. Alberta's assertion that perhaps God took Isabelle so that he would become a priest.

As they reached the overlook at the back of the mission the two stopped and sat together on a huge stone. Fr. Pablo spoke for the first time,"Ferdinand, he said, "First let me address that which I feel you already know is ridiculous, but as a priest had suggested it, I, as a priest, would like to say that it is absurd. God loves you very much, and God loves Isabelle very much. If you discerned that God wanted you to be together, I have no doubt that you were right. I don't blame Diego for wanting to strike Fr. Alberta, if I had been there I might have been tempted myself."

"Thank you," Fr. Pablo, "I have always thought that he was terribly wrong, but it is certainly good to hear it confirmed by a priest that I trust.

"Secondly, you are right on target with the way that you are proceeding with your discernment. If you had come to me before you started trying to discern, I would tell you to do exactly what you are doing, pray, think, and most importantly dedicate yourself to helping others. Ferdinand, you are truly wise beyond your years. Have you ever heard of the Buddha?"

"I know that he is the founder of an Asian religion. I learned that in school, but of course, we are Catholic and so we didn't learn about his specific teachings," replied Ferdinand.

"One of the things that Buddha said that I like is, "If you light a lamp for someone else, it will also brighten your path," said Fr. Pablo."Ferdinand, you have been lighting lamps for other people your whole life. Keep praying, keep helping others, keep thinking and talking to people you trust. Continue to have faith and be patient, and I will give you a couple of books that I think might be helpful. I will pray for you and your discernment, but there is something that I think that I should make clear to you."

"Sure," replied Ferdinand, "What's that?"

"Ferdinand," began Fr. Pablo, "I think that it is important that you know that what you are attempting to discern is whether or not you are being called to the ordained ministry as a priest, not if you are being called as a priest."

"I am not sure that I get it," replied Ferdinand.

"You were baptized priest, prophet, and king," explained Fr. Pablo, "All Christians are. But you have been living out your priestly calling for many years now to a degree that most people do not accomplish in a lifetime. You carried out your priestly duties when you chose to love and forgive Juan as Jesus would have done. You lived your priestly life when, through sharing your faith with Isabelle, you helped her move closer to Jesus and Mary in advance of her heavenly reward. You lived out your priestly calling when, after losing the woman you loved, you devoted your working life to helping your two best friends be together in love. You live out your priesthood through your work in the orphanage, and you certainly lived it out in freeing nine enslaved people and Tianna. I am honored that you have come to me for advice, and I will certainly guide you to the best of my ability, but I think that you should know that in many ways it is I who has been inspired by you."

"Thank you for the kind words, Fr. Pablo," said Ferdinand, "Are you saying that there is not really all that much difference between everyone's baptismal call to priesthood, and the ordained ministry?'

"Not at all," replied Fr. Pablo,"The difference is significant, to say the least. I believe that my call to the ordained priesthood is the greatest gift God has given me next to God's love and my life. If you are called to that life, if that is what God wants for you, then by all means, let nothing get in your way. I will do everything in my power to make sure that you get into the finest seminary, and will support you through your studies. You will make an unbelievable priest, if that is what God is calling you to do. The sacrifices of living the life of an ordained priest are tremendous, but nothing in comparison to the rewards. I merely want to make sure that you realize that God is definitely calling you to a life of service. Your challenge is to find out if it is as an ordained priest or not."

"That you, Fr. Pablo," your insights are wonderful, "It helps to view things in a different light, and I had never thought about ministry this way before. Can I ask you how long the discernment process should take?"

Fr. Pablo laughed, "You can ask, but there is really no set answer to it. The Spirit moves as the Spirit wills. Some people receive answers to the questions very quickly, for others it might take weeks or months or even years. You must be patient and trust God, but believe me, Ferdinand, when you know, you will know you know."

CHAPTER FORTY-EIGHT

"Genuine Christian experience must always include an encounter with God Himself. "

AIDEN WILSON TOZER

That night, for reasons that he did not know, Ferdinand just could not get to sleep. After tossing back and forth for a while, Ferdinand gave up on waiting for rest to come. As quietly as he could he slipped from his bed, careful not to disturb Diego, and walked out of his hut. The night was bright with a full moon and stars dancing throughout the sky. A warm ocean breeze messed with his hair. He found himself sitting on the same rock that he and Fr. Pablo had sat on earlier in the day.

Although it was late and he had been up since early morning, instead of feeling tired he was somehow invigorated by the beautiful evening and the sounds of the waves crashing against the shore. He was, however, tired of thinking about his future. For the first time since Isabelle's death, he decided to let go. "Father," he whispered out loud, "Here I am Lord, I have come to do you will," he said quoting scriptures and then he became quiet.

Suddenly a feeling of calm came over Ferdinand and he

felt a presence all around him, he remembered the feeling he and his friends shared that night outside of Isablelle's house, but this feeling was even deeper and more blissful. He neither talked or thought about anything during the encounter, he simply sat and enjoyed the presence. When it had passed he knew what he was called to do and he knew that he knew it. He went to bed and fell into a deep sleep. When he awoke he felt rested and full of peace and energy.

The next morning was Sunday. Ferdinand and Diego were scheduled to leave the mission on Wednesday, so that they would be ready to sail again on Thursday. Even though Diego was enjoying his time in the mission, he was excited to be starting his return trip in just a few days. He knew he would still have at least seven weeks before they were even docked in Spain, but somehow the thought that he would be actually moving toward Rosalie and the next chapter of his life was exciting to him.

When Diego and Ferdinand entered the chapel, Fr. Pablo was on the altar making preparations for the mass. After genuflecting, they slid into a pew towards the front. A few seconds later, Tianna, imitating the boys as closely as she could, did her own version of a genuflection and slid into the pew next to them. Looking down from the sanctuary, Fr. Pablo"s face displayed a combination of surprise and gladness.

Ferdiand became totally engrossed in the mass. Fr. Pablo was an excellent speaker who gave a homily on the importance of, "Preach the Gospel always, and when necessary use words," a saying often attributed to the Italian twelfth century saint, Francis of Assisi. He spoke of how there are no writings of the priest with the phrase, but whether or not it was accurately attributed to the man, the phrase describes how the saint lived his life. He talked about how it is important for everyone to follow St. Francis' example. He talked about people who spoke the Gospel loudly, but lived lives of hate, and the damage that they brought to the Kingdom of God. It was a very short but powerful sermon.

After mass, Ferdinand again asked Fr. Pablo if they could talk, and of course Fr. Pablo was more than happy to do so. As they walked, Ferdinand began by complimenting Fr. Pablo on his homily. "Thank you," said Pablo, "Many of my best sermons, like today's, come on the spur of the moment."

"You mean that wasn't the sermon that you prepared? What changed your mind?"asked Ferdinand.

"Tianna did," replied Fr. Pablo.

"I saw your surprise when she came into the chapel," said Ferdinand. "Was that the first time she has come?"

"Yes," answered Fr. Pablo, "At least the first time she came willingly on her own. Fruga started to come a couple of years ago, but Tianna never wanted to attend. I encouraged Fugra not to make her. As you know when she was only eight years old, Tianna's life was ripped apart, her father was murdered and unspeakable acts were committed against her mother and other loved ones right in front of her. The perpetrators of these crimes called themselves Christians. It is a tribute to Tianna that she isn't full of hate for all Christians or white people for that matter. I and all of us who minister here have been trying to be the true face of Christ for her since she arrived. Perhaps your and Diego's example, the example of people her own age, was what she needed to see what it really means to be a Christian. I believe that it is too soon to say that Tianna has converted to Christianity, but I believe that she is a step closer and more open to the idea"

"I will keep her in my prayers,"replied Ferdinand.

"Thank you,"said Fr. Pablo, "I appreciate that, but I am guessing that you didn't ask to see me to talk about my homily?"

Ferdinand described in great detail the encounter that he had experienced the night before and the epiphany that he had after it was over. Fr. Pablo listened carefully and assured Ferdinand that his experience was real. "I am happy for you, that you have received the answers which you were seeking,"said Fr. Pablo. "What God is asking of you, will require much sacrifice of you, but following God's will certainly brings many more rewards than sacrifices."

"But what about you Fr. Pablo? I don't want to be presumptuous," said Ferdinand.

"No, no, no,"said Fr. Pablo, "I am thrilled. I will write a letter and ask CookE to deliver it when he gets back to Spain, and we will begin the process."

CHAPTER FORTY-NINE

"We'll be friends forever, won't we Pooh?" "Maybe even longer."

A. A. MILNE

After dinner and the evening campfire, it was Diego who Ferdinand invited to walk so that they could talk. Predictably, the two stopped and sat at the same overlook where Ferdinand had experienced his encounter with God the night before. "I imagine that you are anxious to begin your trip back to Rosalie?" said Ferdinand as a way of making small talk before sharing his plans with his best friend.

"You have no idea how much," responded Diego. "I know that she will also be thrilled to see you."

Ferdinand looked at him with a pained expression on his face. "What?"asked Diego, his mind spinning.

"Listen," said Ferdinand, "You of course know that I have been trying to discern what God wants of me for my future. I have been praying, meditating, and talking with Fr. Pablo."

"Sure," said Diego, "And I hope that you know that I have been praying for you."

"I do, and I appreciate your prayers," said Ferdinand. "Last night on this very spot, I had a special experience. I had an encounter that I know to have been a revelation from God. Afterwards, I was blessed with clarity that I had never had. I knew for certain that I am being called to serve Jesus and his Mother right here, as part of this wonderful ministry. Tianna and I had been talking about how it would be beneficial to separate the younger children from the older students so that the mission can offer more classes and extend the schooling longer for the students. Fr. Pablo is sending word to Spain asking for an upper school curriculum. I will work with the older students and Tianna will work with the younger students."

Diego had trouble swallowing the way a person who is trying to smile and not cry at the same time often does. "I am so happy for you, my friend," he said. "I won't pretend that I won't miss you terribly as will Rosalie and of course your family. If this is what God wants you to do, and I know that you are sure that it is, then the sacrifice will be great —for you and us — but your life will be blessed in so many ways. You know I will support you, as will Rosalie and your family. We all love you."

"I know," said Ferdiand who was now trying to hold back tears. "Over the next two days I will write letters to my family and Rosalie, and ask you to deliver them for me. I will write letters to you and them every chance that I get. I don't need to tell you, Diego, that you are my best friend. I don't want anything to change that."

"I don't think that anything ever could," said Diego. "What about Captain Sanchez, will he be okay with you staying behind?"

"Fr. Pablo said that he would send a letter with you to Captain Sanchez explaining that he has hired me. He said that Captain Sanchez supports the mission and won't have a problem with it, he also said that there are plenty of young men willing to take my spot in exchange for passage back to Europe."

"I have written two letters for you," said Ferdinand, handing Diego two pieces of paper. "The first letter authorizes Captain Sanchez to pay you that which he owes me for the voyage here. The second one releases the funds which I have been saving for you and Rosalie to you. I hope that these funds along with the ones you have made and saved will be enough for you and Rosalie to start your lives together. I know you. I know how hard you work, how smart you are, and how much you love Rosalie. I don't think it will be very long at all before you are out of the living quarters above the store and into your own house."

"I have to speak with Rosalie, but I don't think that will be the plan anymore,"said Diego.

"What do you mean?"asked Ferdinand.

"Well you are right about me working as hard and as smartly as I can to make our shop the best it can be. I am confident that it will be a success. However, I am no longer in such a hurry for us to move into our own house, maybe when we have several kids we will have to, but not anytime soon. I know that Rosalie will agree that it will be more important for us to support our town orphanage and the Santa Maria Mission than getting our own house. As Rosalie said, wherever we are together will be home."

Ferdinand smiled as he remembered what Fr. Pablo had said about all Christians' call to live out their priestly calling and was amazed at the thought of just how well his friends and family lived theirs, and how blessed he was. The two sat on the rock for a couple of hours, dreaming about the future and talking about the past. They even continued the conversation in their beds until the early morning hours.

CHAPTER FIFTY

"For some moments in life there are no words."

DAVID SELZER

That Monday and Tuesday was a blur as Ferdiand and Diego prayed, played and worked hard. Diego, noticed just how happy his friend was as he interacted with his new life here. He knew that he had truly listened to God, and had made the right decision.

On Wednesday morning, the entire mission gathered into the small church as Fr. Pablo blessed Diego, before sending him off on his long mission home. He also prayed for his future life with Rosalie, and thanked him for his courage and dedication to the mission and for his part in saving Mafu and his family.

After the blessing the entire group formed a line outside the doors to bid him farewell. Several of the "wee people" were upset to see their fun-loving buddy leaving. Mafu and his family were at the end of the line. Each family member hugged Diego and expressed their gratitude using the Spanish words that they knew. Then Fr. Pablo, Fruga, Tianna, and Ferdinand walked Diego to the bottom of the steps leading from the mission. The others then stopped and Ferdinand walked with Diego to the beginning of the forest. Before disappearing into the woods, Diego turned and he and Ferdinand embraced for a long time.

Then Diego turned and continued on his journey. Neither of them spoke. They didn't need words. Both knew each other so well they knew what each other was feeling. They knew it was the same as they were feeling, and they were sad and happy and sad and happy for each other.

As Ferdinand neared the others, Fr. Pablo and Fugra turned and began to ascend the steps, while Tianna waited for Ferdinand. As they began to climb the steps behind them, Ferdiand reached out and grabbed Tianna's hand. As he looked over, he saw first surprise and then happiness on her face. Ironically Ferdinand first felt joy that she so happily let him place his hand in hers, and then he felt surprise. "What had given him the idea to do that?" he thought. He had not planned it, and he was not impulsive. His mind traveled back to the first time Isabelle placed her hand in his, and then he remembered the last words she had written to him in her letter.

> *" I will never forget the first time I grabbed your hand and felt your hand in mine. I somehow knew in my heart that we were embarking on something special. Talk to me if you like. I may not be able to answer in a traditional way, but I will always be there for you, and I will always love you. Be open to my prompting and the prompting of our Mother. I promise I will never really leave you.*

"Thank you," whispered Ferdinand as he looked up to heaven.

Made in the USA
Columbia, SC
17 May 2021

38128651R00098